Texas Two-Step
Cowboy Rough Book Five

by

Darah Lace

This is a work of fiction. Names, characters, places, and incidents are either the product of the author's imagination or are used fictitiously, and any resemblance to actual persons living or dead, business establishments, events, or locales, is entirely coincidental.

Texas Two-Step ~ Copyright 2024 by Darah Lace

All rights reserved. No part of this book may be used or reproduced in any manner whatsoever without written permission of the authors except in the case of brief quotations embodied in critical articles or reviews.

Cover Art by Diana Carlile
http://www.designingdiana.blogspot.com

Published in the United States of America

Chapter One

My dick gets hard just thinking about your beautiful tits.

Texas groaned as she read the text and laid her phone face down on the bar. As a child, words like those had instilled fear. More than once, her mama had said bad words would get her mouth washed out and her hide tanned. But now, lord have mercy, those words stirred something else entirely.

"What?" Will Sanderson sat on the stool next to her, his dark brows drawn in a tight frown over brown eyes that watched her a little too closely, as if he could hear the rapid beat of her pulse and knew it centered between her legs.

"Nothing." Ignoring the tingle in her breasts and the tug in her lower belly, she took a drink of her beer and shrugged off the text, one of a dozen she'd received the last few days. Each more graphic than the one before, she'd been in a constant state of arousal. She'd called the guy sending the messages and told him he had the wrong number, but they just kept coming.

Wish I could.

With a mental sigh, she focused on the man who'd been her rock more times than she could remember and tried to think of something other than her need for sex. "You got a good price for your bull."

"Yeah, I did okay."

His spur of the moment addition of fifty head of cattle to today's sale had thrown her. That and the sudden private sale earlier this week of his prize-winning bucking bull. Crusher was Will's pride and joy and had earned the Double A Ranch a hefty purse last year. He was sure to have done the same this year. She couldn't imagine why Will would want to sell the big guy. Unless he needed the money.

"Is everything okay? With the ranch, I mean."

"The ranch is fine." He turned to face the mirror again, his gaze catching hers then flitting away to follow the couples on the dance floor.

She twisted on the high-back stool to see who he might be checking out, but the crowd was a little thin and a lot older tonight except for the newly elected sheriff, Harper Quinn, and her deputies. Texas and Harper had become friends shortly after Harper's arrival back in January, but Texas didn't want to intrude. Dispatch Officer Kelsey Price had passed the state licensing examination to become a Peace Officer, the first step on her way to becoming a deputy sheriff, and they were celebrating.

Texas looked at Will again. Nah, Harper was taken. She and Josh McNamara were engaged and planning their wedding, and hooking up with women in committed relationships... That just wasn't Will's style.

Which, come to think of it, she wasn't quite sure

exactly what his style was anymore. He hadn't dated anyone since he and Krystal split up a couple of months back. Not for lack of willing women. Will was a catch—good-looking, wealthy, a generous heart, and a sense of humor. But he hadn't looked twice at anyone, at least not that Texas had seen.

She and Will had been friends since they were kids, chasing each other through the auction barn her father had passed to her four years ago. She'd thought there might be something between them as teenagers, but an awkward kiss had put an end to that. They'd moved on, maintaining a bond over time that withstood boyfriends and girlfriends and separations while one or the other attended college.

Up until three weeks ago, they'd gone months, almost seven, without a night out. This was the third Saturday in a row they'd met for a beer and to shoot the breeze after she closed up the barn. It felt good, relaxing, comfortable. She'd really missed this, missed Will.

Her phone chirped again, making her skin sizzle. The only one who ever texted her was Will, and his phone was in his back pocket. Her hand trembled as she flipped it over and angled it toward her so he couldn't see.

Anonymous: *I want to lick your nipples.*

Warmth threaded from the hardening tips of her breasts to her belly and then lower. Some woman was going to get very lucky tonight.

"I like the new auctioneer." Will cut into her thoughts.

"Huh? Oh, yeah." Texas lowered her phone and

laughed. Even to her, it sounded false. "He's a little wet behind the ears, but then no one could replace JD. I think he'll work out, though."

Another text sent her phone dancing. She wouldn't look, not this time. Instead, she crossed her legs and squeezed her thighs tight. Wrong move. The thick seam of her jeans only stimulated the sensitive clit.

She uncrossed her legs and picked up her beer. Tipping back the longneck, she drained the bottle dry and signaled the bartender for another. He plunked one down beside her three empties as the phone went off again.

Will paused, his beer resting against his lips, and cut his eyes at her. "Am I keeping you from something? Or someone?"

A cold shower. Or a steamy one with a long soapy orgasm. "Nope."

Chirp. Chirp.

She grabbed her phone, and a searing rush of need spread down her thighs.

Anonymous: *My dick aches to slide slow and deep into your pussy.*

Anonymous: *Mmm, baby, so hot and wet.*

Anonymous: *Can you feel the stretch as I fill you with my cock?*

"Shit." She choked on the word as her core clutched at the imaginary shaft the text brought to mind.

Will lowered his bottle to the bar without taking a drink. "Something wrong?"

"No, it's just this guy." Damn, how could

someone she didn't even know arouse her this much? She had to stop reading the texts. They weren't meant for her, not really.

"Is he bothering you?"

Bothering? More like hot and bothered.

"He's..." Should she tell Will about her sexy mystery texter? He'd probably laugh. But maybe voicing the situation would make her laugh, too, and defuse the hormones running rampant through her body and firing up her libido. "Some guy is sending me these texts, and they're a little on the crude side and—"

"Let me see." He reached for her phone, but she held it away. He sure didn't look amused. In fact, he looked pissed.

"I told him he had the wrong number."

Will leaned into her, his chest flattening her against the back of the chair. She shoved at him, afraid he'd feel the stiff points of her breasts, but he was unbudgable.

"Give me the damn phone." His voice was gruff, his grip tight on her forearm as he swiveled her around and pried the phone from her fingers.

She slapped at his hand but had no choice other than to relinquish the phone. "What are you, two?"

Settling back in his chair, Will ignored her and punched the buttons on her phone until the texts popped up on the screen. "Goddammit, T." He hit Call and, shoving his sun streaked brown hair from his eyes, glared at her. "Listen, dickhead, you're sexting the wrong number, and if you don't stop harassing my wife, I'm going to hunt you down and slice off your balls. Got it?" A slight pause and then, "See that you don't."

Texas snapped her mouth shut, which had dropped open when he'd called her his wife. Where had that come from? And why did it make her feel all mushy?

He handed her the phone. "You don't have to put up with that shit."

The grumbled accusation made her grind her teeth. "You sound like it's my fault. I already told him he had the wrong number."

"Sorry." Remorse flickered in his chocolate eyes. "The idea of some asshole talking to you that way doesn't sit well."

One thing she'd been able to count on over the years was Will's protective nature. Maybe she shouldn't have told him about the texts. They were the most excitement she'd had in years, and now, he'd gone and scared the guy off. "Yeah, well, to be honest, it's times like this I really miss Jarod. I haven't had sex in months."

Will made an unpleasant face as if he had a mouth full of bitters. A hot flush warmed her cheeks. Damn diarrhea of the mouth.

She lifted her beer to her lips. "Sorry, TMI."

Jarod hadn't been a bad boyfriend. He'd been attentive when necessary, scarce when she needed him to be, and he was good enough in the sack. But good enough hadn't been good enough.

"The texts excited you?"

Texas darted a glance at Will and found his gaze drifting over the front of her T-shirt. There went her nipples again. God, she might as well put up a billboard. *Step Right Up Boys. Texas Tallulah Taylor Is Hot & Horny.*

There was no reason to deny his question when the evidence stared right back at him. Texas sighed and twirled the longneck in circles. "Guess you think I'm some kind of a pervert."

He looked away and took another drink. "Why would I think that?"

"I don't know. Just feels wrong or at least like something I should keep to myself."

The big shoulder nearest her lifted and dropped. "Nothing wrong with sexting…if you're careful."

Well, that wasn't the reaction she'd expected. "Are you speaking from experience?"

He gave her another shrug. "Krystal used to be into it."

Figures. Beautiful, vivacious, with a kittenish quality Texas called dumb and needy, Krystal was the kind of woman who could draw men like bees to flowers. She'd always thought Will could do better and was relieved when they'd finally called it quits. But then he'd fallen into a dark, brooding mood.

She'd hoped spending time with him would help yank him out of whatever had him by the balls. For the most part it seemed to work, but there were moments, like now…

A change of subject was called for, but first she had to ask, "Were you? Into it?"

The same dismissive shoulder rose and fell, and she couldn't stop from mentally measuring the width from one to another. All that hard ranch work had kept him in shape. "Until I checked her phone and saw she'd been group sexting."

"What's that?" Man, she was out of touch with the world. She needed to get out more. Or at least start watching reality TV and surfing the net.

"She was sexting me and three other guys. Explained where she was when she wasn't with me, and I couldn't reach her."

Stupid bitch. "I never did like her."

"I know."

"Sorry. I didn't think it showed."

"It didn't, but I know you." He chuckled. "Least I thought I did. Tex the sext addict."

Another scorching blush spread down her chest and arms, and she looked away, feeling defensive. "It's about more than the arousing speech or the naughty images it brings to mind."

"How so?"

She took a page from his book and gave her shoulder a shrug. "His texts were random, night and day, and not just about sex. The idea of a guy being that into a woman, thinking about her that way in the middle of the afternoon, wanting her so much he can't think of anything else…makes me really hot but a little sad, too."

"Why?"

"Because I'm thirty years old and I've never had that. No one has ever wanted me that much." God, she was drunk, talking way too much. But this was Will, and if she couldn't tell him how she felt, she couldn't tell anyone.

"If a man wanted you like that, what would you

want him to say?" His gaze met hers in the mirror and held a seriousness in those dark eyes she hadn't seen in a long while. Almost a sadness.

"I don't know. What would *you* say?" The question came out in a breathless whisper, and his gaze dropped to her mouth. She licked her lips, conscious of their sudden dryness.

His attention returned to his bottle as if the label would tell him what to say. Was it so hard to think of her in those terms? Dammit, they weren't brother and sister.

"Maybe I'd say you have damned kissable lips."

"That's it? That's all you've got?" No wonder Krystal was group sexting. But what did she expect. This was Will, her friend, not her lover. "Hope you're better at sex than sexting."

Beer sprayed from Will's mouth, and he began to choke.

Shit, she needed duct tape over her lips. Grabbing a napkin from the stack in front of them, she dabbed at his chin with one hand and pounded him on the back with the other. "Sorry, I'm over my limit tonight. Can't control what comes out of my mouth."

Will took the napkin from her and wiped the front of his shirt. The bartender came over to clean up the counter. She slid off the high stool. "Time to call it a night."

With one last cough, Will stood, pulled out his wallet, and dropped a few bills on the bar top, enough to cover his tab and hers with a generous tip. He grabbed his Stetson from the stool to his right and crammed it on his head. "Right behind you."

The Rusty Nail, though on the small side, was the hangout for the local ranching community because it sat next door, give or take a quarter mile, to the auction barn. Most of the locals walked over after Texas closed up the barn following the Saturday auction. The older folks talked about the sales and who'd gotten the best deals. The younger set danced, drank, and looked for an available hookup, not that the options were large, but the drive into the city was a long one.

Looks like it was worth the gas money tonight.

Texas walked the worn trail, aware of Will behind her. And more than aware of the four beers making her a little less than steady on her feet. He was quiet, but that was Will, not much for words. She wasn't either. She'd never been one of those women who chattered and tittered about men, fashion, or who was sleeping with whom. Livestock and the price of beef. That's what she talked about. No wonder the men around here never sexted her.

With a sigh, she glanced up at the twinkling stars and nearly toppled over. Will's big hands spanned her waist, holding her upright until she regained her balance. He didn't let go but shifted her under his arm and pulled her close. She leaned into him, grateful for his support and his warmth. Which didn't make much sense since it was a humid summer night.

The gravel of the barn's parking lot crunched under their boots as he steered her around the big red building. They neared his four-door pickup parked out back, and she was surprised when he didn't stop but kept walking toward the house she'd grown up in, only a stone's throw from her livelihood.

"I'll walk you up," he said as if he'd heard her thoughts. Or had she spoken out loud again?

The oak trees around the house cast them in shadow. She'd forgotten to leave the porch light on but knew the path well, even tipsy. So did Will. They stepped in sync over the broken cement jutting several inches out of the ground.

At the top step of the porch, she straightened to dig in her front pocket for her keys. "Got 'em."

Jangling them at him to show her success, she pulled open the screen door. It took her a moment to get the key in the lock, but she managed and the tumblers clicked.

She turned to thank him. "Goodni—"

He stood close, too close, his big frame crowding her space. She glanced up at him, but it was too dark to make out his expression. The hand at her waist pushed her against the door. His head lowered. Warm breath teased her lips, and the slight scent of beer tickled her nose.

"Will?" She barely got the question out before his lips brushed hers softly, lightly. Her tummy took a slight tumble. Then his mouth opened over hers, his tongue moving in slow to skim hers, and the tumble turned into a high-rise free fall.

A low groan rumbled in his throat. His other hand palmed the back of her head as his hips ground into hers. The hard bulge prodding her belly inflamed her arousal. She arched against him, aching for the hand on her ribs to cover her breast, aching for his muscular thigh to slide between her legs.

His tongue eased from her mouth, and his lips were gone, along with the weight of his body. The last to leave were his hands as he stepped back and adjusted the hat cocked to one side of his head. He cleared his throat. "Sorry."

She wasn't. Like the kiss they'd shared fourteen years ago, this one rocked her world. But unlike that kiss, this one had also rocked her pussy. She hadn't thought about stopping him, not for a second. Wished he'd do it again. "Too much alcohol."

"Yeah, and talk of sex."

"Huh? Oh, yeah." Definitely.

He backed up to the edge of the porch. "See you Monday night."

"Monday?" God, she sounded like an idiot. What was it they said about alcohol and brain cells?

"Town meeting, remember?"

Texas groaned. Maybe she'd get drunk again Monday night so she'd have an excuse not to go. "I hate those things."

"Me, too." Will pivoted on the ball of one boot and took the steps two at a time. "Night."

"Night." Texas watched him for a second, that sauntering walk unmistakable, then sighed and let herself in the house. She shut the door, leaned against it, and traced her lips with fingers that shook.

No doubt about it, William Charles Sanderson had kissed her for the second time in her life. And once again, he'd apologized.

"Face it, Texas. Your kisses just don't do it for him." Angry for caring, she pushed off the door, wove across the foyer, and paused at the bottom of the stairs to shuck her boots. Her T-shirt came off halfway up and landed on the floor in the hall.

At the door to her bedroom, she leaned against the jamb and somehow peeled her jeans over her hips and to her ankles without falling flat on her ass. She kicked them to the side and, in just her bra and panties, followed the beam of moonlight slashing across the room to her bed.

Sitting at the foot of the mattress, she flopped to her back and stared at the ceiling. Why should she care if Will liked kissing her? She didn't. Not like she had back then when she'd harbored a young girl's crush on her best friend.

Besides surprising the hell out of her, that youthful uncoordinated kiss against the side of her house had battered every emotion in her blossoming body, tapping into feelings she hadn't understood and sucking the air right out of her lungs.

But the look on his face when he'd ended the kiss...the disappointment and then the obvious discomfort. He'd fumbled through an apology, and she'd let him off the hook, telling him it was for the best they got that out of the way and could focus on simply being friends. She'd learned how to hide her feelings, faster and faster with every girl he dated, until they faded. Eventually, the hurt stopped and she'd moved on, too.

Thank god she wasn't in love with him this time

because he'd obviously had practice, and lots of it. Damn, he was one hell of a kisser. And if he fucked as good as he kissed —

A loud chirp from the heap of denim on the floor drew her attention. Probably the sexting asshole again.

Texas giggled at the thought of Will's face when he'd told the guy he'd castrate him if he texted again. She wouldn't tell, of course. Not when the guy's sex texts made her hot.

Chirp. Chirp

She should ignore her phone and go shower, sober up, and get some sleep. Then again, maybe Asshole would take her mind off Will's kiss and the way his big, hard body had mashed her against the door.

She snorted. That wasn't the only thing big and hard, so he couldn't claim he didn't like her kisses.

"Nope, can't think about Will. Go for the asshole. He's safer."

Chirp.

"Okay, okay." Texas sat up, scrambled to grab her jeans, and wove her way back to the bed. She pulled out her phone and swiped the screen. Four texts. Not from Asshole.

Will: *Hey.*
Will: *You there?*
Will: *Still awake?*
Will: *Guess not. Talk tomorrow.*

"Not very patient. What if I had to pee?" And now that she thought about it…

She laughed and thumbed a message.

Texas: *Wait a sec. Gotta pee.*

A laughing emoji came back immediately.

Leaving the phone on the bed, she teetered to the bathroom, took care of business, and took a minute to wash her face and brush her teeth. She stuck her tongue out at her reflection. The alcohol buzz was still on medium, and her teeth felt kind of numb.

Another chirp drew her back to the bedroom. She picked up the phone, threw back the covers, and crawled to the middle of the queen-sized bed to sprawl on the cool sheets. Only when she was comfortable did she check to see what Will wanted. He deserved to wait for adding to the lust she'd dealt with all week.

Will: *Did you fall in?*

Texas rolled her eyes, which made her head swim and the letters on her phone a bit hard to focus on.

Texas: *Haha. What's up?*

Will: *Just wanted to tell you I lied to you earlier.*

That got her attention. Will didn't lie and never to her.

Texas: *Yeah? What about?*

A minute passed, then another. What could be so wrong that he didn't want to tell her? Was he sick, dying? The thought was sobering. Not her Will.

Losing her mother when she was thirteen to Leukemia had devastated her. Her father's heart attack four years ago had come out of the blue and left her hollow. But if Will—

The chirp of his text startled her, and she nearly

dropped the phone.

Will: *You're lips aren't kissable.*

She blew out a breath. *He isn't sick.*

But the relief she felt didn't even have time to kick in before hurt slammed into her. So he didn't like the kiss. She knew he didn't. He wouldn't have apologized and blamed it on the sex talk. Still, having him say it hurt. A lot.

And what was she supposed to say to that? She texted the only thing she could think of.

Texas: *Ok*

Just as she hit send, another message popped on the screen.

Will: *They're fuckable.*

Texas blinked at the naughty word in the little blue bubble, then checked to make sure the text was from Will and she hadn't accidentally switched to the conversation with Asshole. Nope, Will's picture was right there to the left of the balloon that said "*fuckable.*"

He thought her lips were fuckable? Will?

Her tongue slid across the cracked skin of her bottom lip. The thought of taking his cock in her mouth shouldn't have excited her, but damn if the fiery need in her pussy didn't burn hotter. Her head struggled to tamp down what she told herself was wrong. She shouldn't think this way about her best friend. But the overwhelming lust controlling her body, mixed with the lingering effects of alcohol and the lure of the forbidden, chipped away at her resistance.

He doesn't mean it. Not really. He was probably

teasing or trying to make her feel normal about being turned on by the whole sexting thing. Should she reply as if she thought he was joking? Or did he expect her to sext him back?

She'd been aching to join the conversation with Asshole, to let go and live out a fantasy. But this was Will. He wouldn't let it go that far.

He already has.

She reread the text.

Will: *They're fuckable.*

Closing her eyes, she remembered the way he'd stared at her mouth earlier at the bar. He'd never done that before. Maybe he did think about her that way. Or maybe he missed Krystal and her slutty lips, or just sex in general, and needed an outlet as much as she did. He might even be thinking of Krystal as he texted, or of some nameless woman he'd seen somewhere, which was okay. Texas would probably picture the hunk of manly hotness from the last movie she'd seen… What was his name?

And it wasn't as if they'd do more than share a few naughty words. What harm could it do?

Besides lead you down the path to masturbate? Been there before.

Wouldn't be the first time, and wasn't that the plan anyway?

Thumbs poised to respond, Texas quieted the voice of warning. Once the text went out, there would be no turning back. Releasing a long breath, she typed out a message and hit send.

Chapter Two

Will smacked his palm on the steering wheel and looked up at the house he'd walked away from only moments ago. He hadn't wanted to leave, but he hadn't been able to trust himself. As it was, he'd fucked up everything.

He shouldn't have kissed her, and he damn sure shouldn't have sent the text. But goddammit, his cock ached for Texas, and he'd held his peace—and his piece—for too many years. Now that the verbal dam had burst, he sure as hell couldn't stop the flood. What he couldn't say out loud, he would finally say with a text.

His phone pinged, and a rush of air exploded from his lungs. He was afraid to look, to see the words that would shut him down.

T: *Dreaming of a blowjob, are you?*

It took a few hammering heartbeats to register the words, then a smile tugged at his lips, his shoulders relaxed, and the roiling acid in his stomach eased. Non-committal but not a fuck off, either. Okay, he could deal with that.

Reclining the driver's seat, he set his Stetson in the console and laid back against the cool leather for what he hoped would be a lengthy and very sexual exchange.

That's all it could be...for now. It was too early to tell her how he really felt. She wasn't ready.

Instead, he texted back.

Will: *Every man dreams of a bj.*

Before he chickened out, he added...

Will: *Especially from lips like yours.*

He wanted to say *only from your lips, only ever from you.* Slow. He had to go slow.

T: *What's so great about them?*

Fishing? Texas? She wasn't the type...usually.

Will: *Full lush wet. You lick them a lot. Makes me hard.*

A long minute passed, then two. Fuck, so much for going slow.

"Come on, T. Don't stop now." He looked at the image next to the text balloon above his response, her icon from his contacts list. He'd taken the picture last summer at the Fourth of July picnic. She'd been looking up at the fireworks in the night sky, unaware he was even watching her. Her hair was blowing in the breeze, her expression serene, beautiful.

The screen shifted, a new text arriving.

T: *If I suck your dick, what will you do for me?*

Fire zipped along his spine. His cock strained against the metal teeth of his jeans, and he mashed the heel of his hand down its length. Jesus, just reading the dirty words and hearing her voice in them made him want to fist his dick and pump until he exploded.

Wouldn't take long.

As much as he wanted to pursue the blowjob

fantasy, he needed to make this about her. The texts from that dickhead had been about her, or rather his lover, and if the flush on Texas' cheeks was any indication of how turned on she was, that was the route Will had to choose.

He peppered off several texts back to back.

Will: *I was hoping you'd ask.*

Will: *Do you want me to start by sucking your tits?*

Will: *Or can I go straight for your pussy?*

Will: *Cuz I know you'll taste good.*

T: *Mmm, decisions, decisions.*

He laughed, imagining her expression as she weighed her choices.

Ping.

The text shifted as her next message followed quickly, telling him she didn't take long to make up her mind.

T: *I've got it. I'll handle the upper. You take care of the lower.*

A low groan filled the cab of his truck as he looked up at the dark house. She hadn't turned on any lights, and he wondered where she was. In the living room on the couch, unable to make it up the stairs?

Nah, she hadn't been that drunk. He imagined her lying on her bed, naked and pinching her nipples. Or was she still dressed and just yanking his chain, laughing instead of getting off?

Will: *Before we go any further, where are you and what are you wearing?*

T: *LOL bra and panties on my bed.*

His balls inched up a little closer to his groin as

he pictured her in a black lace bra and thong. No, that wasn't Texas. She was practical, probably wearing white cotton briefs and a utility contraption for her sizable tits. Didn't matter. She'd be sexy in anything.

Will: *Take off your bra so I can see you squeeze your tits and pinch those pink nipples.*

They were pink and dime-sized. He'd seen them through her worn nightgown when he caught her by surprise and stopped by for breakfast early one morning a few weeks ago. The boner he'd sported through waffles and bacon stayed with him the rest of the day. But damn it was worth the pain later that night. Jacking off to the image of his cock gliding between those—

Ping.

T: *Kinda hard to text with one thumb :)*

Will: *LOL try.*

T: *If you insist.*

Will: *I do. Want to hear you moan.*

Even with her windows open and his rolled down, he was too far away to hear the soft whimper of pleasure.

T: *Mmmmmmmmmm.*

It wasn't audible, but her texted moan did the trick. Pre-cum leaked from the crown of his throbbing erection, dampening his boxers. Fuck, he wasn't going to last long if he didn't focus on Texas and her needs.

Will: *Feel good?*

T: *Yes.*

The thrumming pulse in his dick increased. Too

much pressure. He popped the button of his fly and lowered the zipper to offer some relief.

Will: *Is your pussy wet?*

T: *Yes, it needs attention.*

Will: *Spread your legs and lift your knees so I can see.*

He waited until she complied, at least in his mind.

Will: *Fuck, that's sweet. Pink and juicy. I'm going to eat you up.*

T: *Yes.*

He wished he could. This game of sexting would never be enough.

Will: *Tastes so good. All that cream.*

He could almost taste it for real. Her scent promised the sweetness of apples and honey. It drove him crazy when they danced. They hadn't done much of that in a while, but as teenagers they'd taught each other, absorbing all the technique of western and ballroom dancing. He'd been afraid the guys at school would find out, but he hadn't been able to resist the chance to hold her body against his.

T: *This isn't working.*

Will sat up slowly, dread washing over him. This was it, the moment he'd feared. She must have sobered up and realized she couldn't get off thinking of him.

Now what, dickhead? She'll start avoiding you, feel uncomfortable around you.

He'd screwed up, moved too fast. This had not been part of his plan at all.

Spending more time with Texas, getting her

used to him again, maybe a date that wasn't a date — a movie, dinner, holding her hand, small touches. Then, after a month or two, when he thought she might be open to it, he'd up his game with a kiss. Sex wasn't on the agenda for months, and here he'd jumped right into it before he even got started.

Driving his fingers through his hair, he pondered what to say. What could he say? *Sorry, but I think of fucking you all the time and couldn't resist a verbal attempt?*

Ping.

T: *This would work better if you were here to do it. I'd be free to text.*

A bark of laughter silenced the buzz of cicadas. Maybe she was drunker than he thought. Logical should have been her middle name instead of Tallulah.

Will: *If I was there, you wouldn't be able to text.*

T: *Is that a threat?*

Will: *It's a promise.*

T: *Don't make promises you can't keep.*

Sassy much?

Will: *Have I ever?*

T: *Hmph. Too bad you're not here to deliver this one.*

Will: *Is that an invitation?*

He knew it wasn't, but that didn't mean he couldn't hope.

T: *Ha! Problem solved. Found the speaker option for texts. Hands-free now.*

Will fell back against the seat with a groan of part disappointment and part lust. He concentrated on the latter and what her text really said. If she was hands-free, did that mean she was actually playing this out? Touching herself to his texts?

Fuck, fuck, fuck. He ached to see her hands on her tits, kneading, fingers rolling those hard tips. Her back would arch off the bed, lips slack, a soft cry escaping them. One hand fisting his hair as he flattened his tongue on her clit.

He fired off instructions.

Will: *Slide one hand inside your panties. Finger that little button. Imagine it's my tongue.*

T: *Thought you were going to handle the bottom.*

Will let out a strangled chuckle.

Will: *I'd love to handle your bottom but since I'm not there…*

While he waited for her to respond—and hopefully comply—he closed his eyes again and eased his hand under the waistband of his boxers. Gripping his cock, he squeezed hard and slid his fist down until the skin around his shaft stretched taut. With the slow glide of his thumb, he traced the slit at the tip, spreading the slippery fluid over the head, imagining it was her hot cream coating him as he probed the mouth of her pussy.

Her reply yanked him from the fantasy.

T: *Wish you were.*

His chest tightened, and his mind whirled. Was it wishful thinking that *her* wish was actually real, seeing as how this was the second time she'd mentioned him being there? And what if he were? Would she let him finish what they'd started or call a halt to the whole damn thing, telling him it was okay on the phone but wrong in person?

He didn't want this to be wrong. What if she didn't either? What if —

Ping.

T: *Not enough. Need more.*

He had to take a chance.

Will: *I can give you what you need.*

T: *Please.*

Will bolted upright and, in seconds flat, was out of his truck and running across the gravel lot. His heart knocked against his ribs as he took the steps of her porch two at a time and tried the door. It wasn't locked; he'd fuss at her later about that. Much later. He hopped over her boots to the third stair and didn't stop until he stood outside her room.

From the door, he saw her, just as he'd imagined all these years. Only better. A thousand times better.

Sprawled on the flowery sheets, her lithe slender body soaked up the moonlight spilling through the window. As he'd pictured, her head craned into the bed, long blonde hair splayed around her. Perfect teeth bit the tender flesh of her plump lower lip. Her back arched off the mattress, breasts, mouth-wateringly large, thrust high.

One hand was at her breast, tweaking the rosy nipple. The other was hidden under hot pink satin. Hot fucking pink!

A soft moan drifted around him, drawing him to the edge of her bed.

Her phone lay face up on a belly flat with grooves that spoke of the toned muscle beneath. Legs that stretched for miles and took a stride nearly matching his own, legs he longed to slip between, were bent at the knees, drawn up, and spread wide. Jesus, she was… "So damn beautiful."

Long black lashes fluttered against her cheeks then lifted. Green eyes the color of a spring meadow were glazed with desire as she lifted her head to look at him under heavy lids. "Please be real."

"Oh, I'm real all right, darlin'." Will reached across the bed, grasped one ankle, and dragged her toward him. With a quick move that revealed the depth of his need for her, if only to himself, he scooped her up and into his arms. Her soft curves melted against him, warning him to go easy as he covered her mouth with his.

Her lips parted, inviting him inside, and he swept his tongue into the hot cavern of her mouth, slow to explore, relishing the sweet taste of Texas. Her tongue danced with his, a sensual mating that stirred the fire in his gut and sent his senses whirling. Damn, he could drown in her kiss.

A shudder racked his body as her hands, rough from hard work at the barn and nothing like those of the pampered women he'd dated, smoothed from his shoulders to the base of his neck. Her fingers threaded through his hair, pulling him closer. She curled one leg around his and ground her pussy against his thigh.

He growled and filled his hands with her silky flesh. Her nothing of a waist, the swell of her hips, the round globes of her ass, he wanted it all, had dreamed of it for so long. Too long to allow common sense any say. Yet someone had to have some.

Drawing on the last shred of self-control he

possessed, Will ended the kiss and rested his forehead against hers, his breath labored and quick.

"No." She squirmed to get closer, though that was impossible while he still had on clothes. She lifted her face for his kiss. "Don't stop."

No, he didn't want to, wouldn't unless she asked. But first… "Are you sure?"

"What? Yes." Texas tightened her grip in his hair and tried to draw him to her lips. The leg wrapped around his thigh rose to embrace his hip, and she tilted her hips to ride the rigid length of his cock.

His hips responded without permission, jerking to meet her slow grind. He took hold of her hands, pried them from his hair, and widened the gap between them to mere inches. "Texas, I need you to be sure."

She looked up at him, and the heat in her eyes, that please fuck me look, was nearly his undoing. "I'm sure, Will. I need you."

Not the three words he wanted to hear, but they were a start, and he thanked his lucky stars for them. Whether she'd had too much to drink or was just lonely, hell, he didn't care. And he didn't care that his plan of going slow had been blown to shit. He couldn't stop now.

****

Through a haze of lust, Texas surfaced enough to watch the gentleman inside Will shut down. Thank god. As much as she loved that part of him, she didn't want it now. Not with need raging so hot and clamoring for relief.

With firm hands, he pressed her to sit on the edge of the bed and stepped out of her reach. She started to complain but realized the distance allowed her to appreciate his strip tease. He was tugging the dark teal T-shirt over his head, and all the carved ridges of a six-pack made her fingers itch to trace them.

She thought she'd been dreaming, her fantasy come to life when she heard his whiskey-deep voice at the foot of her bed. Then she'd opened her eyes to see his big frame painted by shadow and moonlight, and the coiling ache in her core wound tighter, sharper.

The roughened hand around her ankle had felt real enough. And god, the hard body he'd held her against was convincing. But those warm lips slanting over her mouth, they were the kicker. He was no dream. This was Will, in her room, kissing her, his hands roaming her back, the base of her spine, the hollow between her shoulders, crushing her to him in a firm but gentle embrace. Keeping his promise.

"I lied about something else tonight." His voice drew her gaze to his, but only for a second as the whir of his zipper lured it back down. He thumbed the waistband and started to push those ass-hugging jeans over his hips then stopped.

When he didn't continue, she dragged her eyes up the line of fine golden-brown hair above his black boxers, over the expanse of his sculpted chest, tan from the hot summer sun, and finally to the face so familiar to her yesterday yet such a mystery tonight.

Her tummy did one of those weird little flips she'd felt earlier.

Knowing he waited for her to acknowledge his confession and wouldn't continue until she did, she said, "Twice in one night? That's not like you, Will."

He smiled and damn if she didn't melt. "Maybe you don't know me as well as you think."

Obviously. His actions tonight weren't anything like the Will she'd grown up with, depended on, shared all the good and bad with. He'd certainly never shown her this aggressive sexual side. It was a little scary. But not enough to make her want to stop. "So, what did you lie about?"

He chuckled and, bending at the waist, pushed his jeans down, down, down those long legs. He kicked his jeans aside then ripped off his socks. When had he taken off his boots? Why the hell did she care when the center of attraction bobbed in front of her at eye level. Thick, ruddy, with veins etching the length, his cock beckoned. Hadn't he said he dreamed of a blowjob?

"I enjoyed the hell out of that kiss." He nudged a boot out of his way. "I want to do it again."

She licked the corner of her mouth but couldn't take her eyes off his erection. He'd said he liked her lips—well, lips like hers, anyway. *They're fuckable.* "What's stopping you?"

"Not a damn thing."

He reached for her just as she slipped to her knees and flattened one palm on his thigh. She curled the fingers of her other hand around the base of his cock. He froze, his muscles going stiff. She spared him a glance, then slipped her lips over the broad head of his cock.

Before she could savor the salty flavor of his essence, he gripped her upper arms and lifted her off the ground.

"I thought you dreamed of a bj."

"Later." The hands on her arms shifted to her waist. A second later, she was flying backward, landing with a soft bounce and a yelp of giddy excitement. Oh, hell yes, she liked this side of Will.

Shoving the hair from her face, she propped on one elbow and glanced up as his knee made contact with the bed. He tossed his wallet to the floor and ripped open a foil packet. The condom rolled quickly down his turgid length, and her pussy spasmed at the thought of him filling her.

Her heart took off in a mad gallop as he dropped to all fours and began a leisurely crawl up her body, like a hungry wolf stalking a quivering rabbit. Instinct had her inching up the bed, but long fingers wrapped around the backs of her knees and shoved her legs apart. One hand on her hip pinned her in place. The other braced his weight, and his head lowered to her breast.

A breath caught in her throat at the first rasp of his rough tongue across her nipple. A cry forced the trapped air out as he closed his scorching hot mouth over the peak of her breast and sucked hard. Streaks of fiery lust threaded from her breast to the depths of her core, swirling, rising with every long draw, creating a whirlpool of desire. Her clit picked up a throbbing pulse in time with her thundering heart.

Texas drove her hands into his thick hair, fisting a handful to bring him closer as she arched into his mouth. "Ahh, Will."

He hummed a response, sending a vibration through her that fueled her already insane lust. She wriggled her hips, grinding her pussy against his rigid abs. When that wasn't enough, she twisted toward the erection prodding her thigh. The hand on her hip pressed her into the mattress and away from her target.

"Please, Will, I need you."

He released her nipple with a soft nip and nuzzled his way through the valley between her breasts and up the other peak. His tongue circled the areola. "Not yet."

But as he took the sensitive tip in his mouth to repeat the sweet torture, his fingers teased their way under the elastic of her panties. His lips feathered the underside of her breast. "Never figured you for hot pink satin, T."

Neither had she, but the erotic texts from Asshole had driven her to buy a set of risqué lingerie. She thought they'd make her feel sexy, but it wasn't the sensuous slide of satin as she'd put them on or the barely-there design molded to her body that made her feel desirable, wanton. It was the way Will looked at her right now.

Slowly, one finger coursed over her mound and sifted into the curls at the top of her folds. Yes.

He groaned and released her breast. "Fuck, you're wet."

Wet? She was drenched. "Yes. I'm ready."

"Not yet." He moved back to the other breast, his teeth grazing, nipping the flesh underneath, his tongue soothing the bites.

As good as it felt, she wanted to scream. What the hell was he waiting for? Then the finger hovering at the top of her pussy slid between slippery lips and found her swollen clit. Her hips jerked away, the nub sensitive to the touch. His finger followed, tapping lightly.

Her head spun as icy-hot pleasure careened down her thighs. "Oh, god."

Tightening the hold on his hair, she flattened her feet against the mattress for leverage and thrust against his elusive digit. He grunted and eased his finger to her slick opening. The slow penetration drew a moan, his withdrawal a whimper. A second finger thickened his next entry, driving deeper, stretching her inner walls, speeding the current of the raging whirlpool threatening to drag her under.

The steady but leisurely in-out rhythm of his fingers and the hard suction of his mouth held her on the brink of orgasm, teasing her with the promise of something stronger, more exquisite than the pleasure coursing through her. If she could get him to alter his angle—

The suction on her breast eased, and his warm lips roamed up her chest to press open-mouthed kisses at the curve of her neck. His breath was hot against her skin, sending shivers back to her pouting nipples.

"You feel so good." His tongue laved the area behind her ear and triggered a shiver. "Like wet silk." His whispered words, thick and raspy with lust, drove her as crazy as the drag of her earlobe through his teeth. "I want that silk wrapped around my dick."

"Yes, Will. Now, please." Begging. She was begging. Never had that happened, not with any of the few lovers in her meager sex life. God, it was wonderful.

"Soon." On the next deep plunge, he curled his fingers to lightly rub that delicious sweet spot, and it was almost enough to send her flying. "Ah, yeah, there it is. You want that again, don't you?"

"Yes."

Again, the briefest touch and the hint of that fiery bliss she craved. Then those evading fingers were slipping away, along with the warmth of his body, leaving her empty and aching. He pried her hands from his hair and sat back on his heels. In a quick, easy move, he peeled off her panties and was hovering above her again.

The head of his cock probed the entrance of her pussy. His lips dipped in to brush hers. "I'm so hard for you I hurt." Another feathery kiss. Splayed fingers framed her face. "Beautiful, so beautiful."

For a brief moment, she opened her eyes. The rampant desire in his sucked the air from her lungs. This Will, this wildly aggressive, sexually confident man was a complete surprise and called to a side of her she hadn't known existed.

With a growl, he swooped in, his mouth possessing hers in an erotically unhurried way that melted her muscles. She became a pliable heap of tingling flesh eager for his talented hands to mold her into whatever he desired. His tongue curled around hers as his cock slowly filled her, its girth much bigger than the two fingers he'd fucked her with moments before.

Needing all of him, she slipped her legs around his and dug her heels into the back of his thighs, urging him deeper. Her urgency did nothing to sway him. Nor did her whimpered plea. Under her palms, the sinewy hardness of his sculpted shoulders gave way to his back as she made her way to the dimples above that gorgeous ass. Her fingernails dug in.

His hips jerked forward, spearing his cock to the hilt. Their lips tore apart in mutual gasps. Another rumbling growl was her only warning before he grasped her wrists and trapped them above her head. She started to complain but his hips rocked back and the delicious friction of his shaft against her cunt had her biting her lip.

"Jesus, Texas...can't wait...need to fuck you." Slanting his lips over hers, he matched the frantic mating of their tongues with the smooth powerful pistoning strokes of his cock. Every drive forward scraped that inner knot of nerves and ground his pubic bone against her clit, shoving her deeper into the spiraling pool, closer to its elusive center. Around and around, closer, closer. Almost there...yes!

Rapture, hot and tingly, spread from her core outward to the tips of her toes and fingers. Even the roots of her hair sizzled. Her muscles locked. A cry ripped from her throat, absorbed by his relentless kiss. As relentless as his fucking. Wave after wave washed over her, and Texas let them—him—carry her away.

Just when she thought she was about to surface, Will shortened and quickened his thrusts. Little bursts of pleasure erupted along every nerve, dragging her back under. He slammed deep. His body tensed. He ripped his mouth away, and a low roar that sounded almost painful echoed in her humming ears. His shaft pulsed, releasing hot semen into the condom as he came with her.

Together they floated until the last spasm passed and her muscles relaxed. His head hung, forehead resting on her shoulder, and his weight settled, pressing her lower body into the mattress. An oddly welcome weight. Comfortable. Safe.

And oh, so wrong.

Chapter Three

Here we go.

Will knew the second Texas stopped feeling and started thinking. Her body went from relaxed to rigid beneath him. The hand drawing lazy patterns on his back stilled.

"Will?"

"Give me a minute."

An hour, the night…the rest of your life.

He wanted to relish the moment, to lay beside her, to fall asleep with her soft body molded to his. But she was on the verge of panic, and if he wanted this to ever happen again, more importantly to make her love him in the process, he had to work fast to keep her off balance until he could come up with a new plan.

Slowly, he eased his semi-hard cock from her tight warmth, but that was as far as he went. He couldn't afford the time or the space between them for a trip to the bathroom to dispose of the condom. Instead, he launched an offense, trailing open-mouthed kisses along her neck to the collarbone and lower.

A shiver shook her, and her nipples puckered as he approached. Her muscles began to loosen.

"Will, wait."

He ignored her and took one rosy peak in his mouth, drawing the taut bud against the roof of his mouth. She jerked, then moaned and arched her curves into him. Fuck, she felt good. He smoothed one hand over the swell of her hip and down the sleek length of her thigh. Hooking a hand behind her knee, he drew her leg higher and around his waist. The slide of her silky skin sent blood rushing to his dick again.

Long slender fingers wove through his hair and tugged. "Will, we can't."

With a loud pop, he released her breast and nipped at the pebbled tip with his teeth. "I'm pretty sure we can," he said, intentionally misunderstanding and letting his hand roam over the rounded curve of her firm but lush ass. "I'm hard as a rock."

"This was a mistake."

Her words cut into his heart like jagged glass, slashing through the emotion he'd kept hidden so many years. Emotion that threatened to spill from his lips. His gut twisted, his throat tightened, and it took every ounce of strength he possessed to keep his words light and pain free. "Best mistake I've made in a while. Let's make it again."

When his teasing earned him a soft laugh, he trailed his fingers along the crease of her ass to her wet center.

"Mmm-mmm-mmm, what have we here?" He grazed her clit with his thumb. "A swollen little button just waiting for me to push." Two fingers glided into her scorching pussy. "No resistance here.

Soaking wet."

He licked a circle around her nipple and curled his fingers in search of her G-spot. She moaned, her inner walls constricted, and moisture trickled to dampen his palm. Without lifting his head, he risked a glance at her. As much as he needed to keep her from over-thinking things, he also needed her to be a hundred percent on board. "Is that a yes?"

Her face contorted in frustration, eyes scrunched shut and teeth digging into her lower lip. Still caught up in her head. A little added pressure of his thumb, and a strangled cry forced her mouth open. "Shit."

He chuckled. "That's what I thought."

"God, Will, we shouldn't do this."

"Again?"

"Yes," she said on a sigh. Whether she meant yes, they shouldn't or yes, do it again, he wasn't sure. But when he scissored his fingers to test her, she jumped "No, I mean no. We have to stop. We've had too much to drink and…"

Will froze, and this time he lifted his head to look her straight in the eye. "You might have had a little too much before I walked you home, but you were sober enough when we started this. We both knew what we were doing, and you said you were sure."

Her gaze darted to the left and settled on his shoulder. "I was, but…"

Fuck, he'd pushed her as far as he could without stepping over the line. "But?"

"Aren't you afraid this will change everything?"

"Do you feel things have changed?" Part of him

hoped she did. Nothing had changed for him. He still loved her as much as he ever had, probably more.

"I don't know. But what if it does? We've been friends for a long time, and if—"

"We still are. That hasn't changed." A new plan formed quickly, and he hoped to god it worked. "And it won't. Not if we don't let it. We can have sex and remain friends."

Those pretty green eyes flitted back to his face, and he read the mixture of fear and desire. "Can we?"

"Just think about it." He withdrew his fingers and plunged them deeper, then circled her clit with his thumb. "Sex when we want, no strings." He ran his tongue over her nipple as he continued to stroke in and out. Her hips lifted to meet each thrust though she kept her eyes on his. "Fun for the taking…wherever…whenever." He wiggled his brows. "I'd be your booty call."

"And I'd be yours." She closed her eyes. "What if you meet someone?"

He wouldn't. She'd never be just an easy fuck to him. But he could use the time with her, the closeness, the intimacy of sex to show her how much he loved her. And hopefully to get her to fall in love with him in the process. He merely needed to convince her to go along with his plan. "If either wants to walk away, we'll go right back like before, just friends."

Silence filled the room except for the wet sounds of his fingers fucking her slick channel. Then her hand, still tangled in his hair, applied gentle pressure to his head and guided his mouth back to her breast.

He didn't hesitate but renewed the worship of her perfect mound with his tongue, sucking hard. Another gush of cream coated his fingers, and the smell of her arousal teased his senses. His balls tightened and fluid leaked from his shaft. He needed to drive his dick deep, to feel her velvety heat surround him. He abandoned her tit and growled as he realized he'd outmaneuvered himself. "I hope to god you've got another condom."

She stretched a hand above her head and to the right. "In the nightstand."

Will withdrew his fingers and grabbed her by the waist to move her farther up the bed then leaned to grab one of two condoms from the drawer and ripped open the packet. He'd have to replenish her supply, and then some, if they were going to have sex as often as he intended. If he had his way, he'd keep her in bed twenty-four/seven.

Before she could change her mind, he stripped the used condom from his straining dick, dropped it over the side of the bed, and rolled on the new one. Deciding to keep things interesting for her—he'd be satisfied with missionary for the rest of his life if it meant having Texas—Will flipped her over and kneed his way between her legs.

A squeal of surprise made him smile as he grasped her hands and wrapped them around the walnut spindles in the headboard. His mouth close to her ear, he whispered, "I'm going to fuck that tight little pussy until you scream."

Backing away, he could have sworn he heard her moan. Who knew his Texas liked the dirty talk? If *he* had known, he might have tried it sooner.

With his hands framing her hips, he hauled her ass in the air and nudged her thighs open, keeping her upper body pressed to the mattress. His cock strained toward her pussy. He gripped himself in one hand and guided the head inside. The shaft followed, and he clenched his jaw to keep from plunging deep as her cunt swallowed him inch by inch.

Fuck, the sight was hot. *She* was hot. And so goddamn wet…tight…a sweet slice of pure heaven. He needed to fuck her — hard, fast, and deep.

"Hold on tight, T. We're going for a ride." He didn't wait for a reply, nor did he take his time as he had earlier. Rearing back, he slammed forward. He ignored her startled cry and repeated the pumping action. Fingers gripping her hips, he held her still as he drove his cock balls deep.

A soft noise drew his attention from the joining of their bodies to her face. A tumble of damp tangles wove a thin veil over her eyes, pale lashes fanned her cheek, and her lips were parted, slack, and dewy. The sound coming from them was a long continuous purr with short bursts as he rammed home and her body took the impact. Unn-unn-unn, like an engine trying to turn over. It shouldn't have been sexy, but it accelerated his lust and compelled him to fuck harder, faster, deeper.

The pitch of her cries rose. She no longer held

onto the spindles. Her hands rested flat near her head as if she didn't care whether or not he plowed her into the headboard. Or maybe she simply left it to him to ensure her comfort and safety. So trusting, so accepting. In his dreams, he'd made love to her a thousand different ways, but this wasn't making love. This was fucking. And yet she didn't seem to mind at all. In fact…

"Somebody likes a hard fuck as much as she likes dirty talk, doesn't she?" Her pussy clenched, and he grunted. "Yeah, T's an naughty girl. She loves a rough ride."

Sweat trailed from his temple to his jaw and dripped onto her ass only to run a meandering path along her spine until it pooled between her shoulders. His breath grew heavy, and his heartbeat drummed in his ears to compete with the slap of wet skin against wet skin.

"Plea-ease."

He barely heard her, but he knew she wasn't asking him to stop. She wanted to come and couldn't at the angle he held her. One slight tilt and she'd go off. But he wasn't done. He'd never be done. If he could last all night, he would.

With that thought came the familiar tingle in his lower spine, the churning in his balls. Fuck, he wasn't ready.

Reaching around her, he found her clit, plump with need. A finger on either side, he started a quick vibrating circular motion, then adjusted her hips so that his cock grazed her G-spot. Her whole body stiffened. A scream sifted past the thundering in his ears, and her pussy locked around his dick, spasming, sucking him deeper with every thrust.

Will tried to keep up the frenzied rhythm, but cum shot from his balls through his shaft in pulsing waves of hot pleasure. His hips jerked, his cock needing to anchor deep inside her. He thrust forward and groaned long and loud as he let go and rode out the storm of his release.

The orgasm ebbed to a faint throb, and he fell to his side, taking Texas with him so they remained joined. She lay limp and motionless except for the rapid rise and fall of her chest. He felt the same, spent, content to close his eyes and savor the moment. But if he was going to convince her nothing had changed and this was a sex-with-no-strings thing, he had to behave as he would with any other lover.

Still, he couldn't make himself get up and go. Not quite yet.

A slight movement shook the bed, and he thought she was crying until he heard the quirky hiccup of laughter that never failed to make him smile. "What's so funny?"

Her laughter stalled, and he was sorry he'd disrupted her humor, but then she hummed. "Nothing. Just thinking about what I said earlier."

Knowing it was best to end the night on a good note and to touch her again as he wanted to would only prolong the leaving, he slipped from her and rolled to his back. He scratched his chest absently. Already he missed her. "What did you say?"

"Oh, just something about the comparison of

your texting abilities to your sexual prowess."

His lips tugged into a grin as he remembered. "I thought I improved your opinion of my sexting abilities."

"True, you did show a great deal of improvement in that area."

"What about the other?" Before tonight, he might have been worried about his performance with Texas, but after her response to his touch and witnessing the powerful intensity of the orgasms he'd given her, he was confident in her answer.

"Krystal was an idiot."

"Hmph." He couldn't disagree, though not for the reason she thought. He didn't want to talk about Krystal, though, or any other ex-girlfriend. They'd only been fill-ins for Texas. And besides, maybe the reason Krystal hadn't been satisfied was because he hadn't either.

Texas surprised Will by rolling toward him and resting her chin on his chest as if she'd forgotten all about her previous reservations. "You're really good at it. Sex."

"I aim to please."

"Yes, you do." She drew lazy patterns over his chest and around one nipple. His abs contracted, drawing her attention lower.

It was too soon to make a full recovery, but he could feel the stirrings of an erection, which reminded him of both the condom on his dick and the one on the floor. Grabbing her hand, he brought it to his lips and kissed the back of her fingers. "As much as I'd love to go for round three, I've got livestock to feed in the morning."

He sat up, and she rose with him to grab the sheet from the foot of the bed. She hugged it to her chest and watched him walk to the bathroom and back again. He liked that, the feel of her eyes caressing his chest, his arms, his ass as he bent to clean the hardwood.

He grabbed his jeans and stepped into one leg then the other but left the zipper undone as he sat on the edge of the bed and put on his socks. "If you keep looking at me like that, there will be a round three."

She drew the sheet tighter. "Sorry. It's just... You have a nice body. I've known you all my life, and I've never really seen it, not naked."

"Nearly naked." He rose to grab his boots. "When we used to swim at the lake." He'd spent many a night wondering about the treasures hiding under those little triangles she called a swimsuit.

"Well, yeah, I mean I knew you had a great body, but I never let myself think of you that way."

"Why not?" He stuffed his head and arms through his shirt then smoothed it over his belly and tucked it into his jeans. "I'm a sexy cowboy, or so I've been told. And I'm good in bed."

Rolling her eyes, Texas fell against the pillows and laughed. "Cocky much?"

When the only thing left to do, buckling his belt, was done, he had to ignore the urge step up to the bed and kiss her goodnight. Instead, he forced his feet toward the bedroom door. "Sweet dreams, Tex."

"Night."

Down the stairs and out the front door—locking it behind him—and as much as he wanted to stay, each step got lighter. He might have screwed up his first plan, but he liked this one a whole hell of a lot better. Sex with Texas had been incredible, and she was already starting to see him in a different light, even if it was only physical. It was a start.

Will climbed into his pickup and drove out of the parking lot happy and satisfied. Definitely satisfied. He grinned.

Yeah, sexting Texas was the best idea he'd ever had.

Chapter Four

Sexting with Will was the stupidest thing Texas had ever done. Unless she counted actually having sex with him.

Pacing the sidewalk outside the town hall, she couldn't make herself go inside just yet. Not even the hundred degree sun baking her skin nor the sweat beading between her breasts could get her in that building. She'd parked beside his truck in the corner of the parking lot. He was already inside and texting her every five seconds.

Will: *Where you at?*
Will: *Saved you a seat.*
Will: *Getting crowded.*

When he left Saturday night, or rather Sunday morning, she must have been riding the high of multiple orgasms. Talking her into this crazy arrangement of sex with no strings had been a breeze for Will and his boyish charm. And god, could he turn it on when the mood suited him.

The question was, why the hell would it suit him? Well, besides the easy lay and a man's basic need to fuck whatever was in front of him. Not that she hadn't enjoyed sex with Will. She'd enjoyed it too much, and now that she had and knew the delights he could make her feel, saying no would be impossible.

One thing gnawed at her, though. If she had this many second thoughts, what could he be thinking? And how could she face him and see the regret or embarrassment in his eyes or, worse, the fear that she'd want to do it again when he'd changed his mind?

Her head swam with possible scenarios of how the next meeting would play out. Why was she worried when his texts indicated all was just fine on his end? He was the same old Will. Sex with her hadn't fazed him one bit. Typical man.

Come on, Texas. You can shake this.

She hated feeling insecure. Odd though, now that she thought about it, she hadn't felt this way since high school, not since she'd kicked her infatuation with Will the first time.

"Hey, Texie."

Will called her T and sometimes Tex, but only one person was allowed to call her Texie, and that was JD Bradburn, the newly retired auctioneer. He'd come with the barn when her dad had taken over thirty-six years ago, and he'd been old and wrinkled way back then. "Hi JD."

The man's spine was hunched, and he might hobble, but his mind was quick and sharp. "I see yer procrastinatin' goin' in. Don't blame you. Wouldn't be here myself if not for talk of the highway expansion."

"Yeah. That's why I'm here." Her barn wasn't affected, but a lot of town businesses were. "Walk me in?"

"My pleasure, young lady." He held out an arm, elbow crooked.

She looped hers through his, and together they braved the madhouse. The second the door opened, the loud buzz of the crowd assaulted her ears. Most were already seated, finding it better to have a place to sit than be forced to stand in the back.

"Looks like a long night of nonsense ahead." JD removed his beat-up straw hat.

Will stood up and waved her over, looking yummy in his red T-shirt and jeans, his wavy brown hair creased from the Stetson he'd probably left in his truck. Her tummy fluttered, and her nerves jangled, but she steered JD in his direction.

JD patted her hand on his arm. "When are you two gonna quit hem-hawing and tie the knot?"

The question caught her off guard and sent blood rushing to her cheeks. What? Was there a sign on her forehead that read *I Fucked Will*? JD couldn't know what they'd been doing, even with the blush touting her sins, but *she* sure did, and the memory came crashing back in vivid images. The warmth in her face arrowed straight between her legs, and her nipples hardened.

This was not good. How would she endure a long night of boring business while sitting right next to Will and having flashbacks of their sexcapades? She cleared her throat if not her dirty mind. "It's not like that between me and Will. We're just good friends."

"If you say so." JD shuffled to a stop. "Hey, Will."

Will stepped out of the row of metal folding chairs to make room for her to claim the seat he'd saved, but as flustered and turned on as she was — oh, hell no, not going to happen.

"JD, you sit with Will." She looked to the rear of the small hall. "I see a spot in the last row."

Without another word, Texas skirted both men as Mayor Radcliff asked everyone to take a seat. She'd lied of course. There was no seat in the back, so she'd have to stand. She glanced around for a place to light. Jarod propped against the wall on the opposite side of the room, and she thought about joining him, but she didn't want to encourage him by seeking him out. The state she was in, best to keep to herself.

"Texas." Sheriff Harper Quinn waved her over. She stood next to Josh opposite Jarod. They scooted over to make room.

"Thanks." Texas leaned against the wall beside Harper and crossed one booted foot in front of the other.

"Standing room only, tonight," Harper whispered.

"The expansion has a lot of people worried," Texas said. "I'm only here because I promised Will."

Harper nodded. "I wish I didn't have to be. Radcliff loves the sound of his own voice."

The vibration of her phone had Texas plucking it from the rear pocket of her jean skirt.

Will: *JD smells like mothballs.*

She tucked her lips between her teeth to keep from smiling and typed a reply.

Texas: *Be nice. JD is family.*

The meeting was called to order and the crowd quieted. Texas listened for a whole three minutes before she tuned out Mayor Radcliff's voice. From her position, she could see the back of Will's head, his shoulders, and part of one long leg stretching into the aisle. He wasn't paying any more attention to the council than she was, with his head down, probably nodding off.

Harper's shoulder nudged Texas' as she leaned close. "You and Will having a good time?"

A flush warming her from head to toe, she stared to Harper. Had she seen Will enter her house Saturday night? "What do you mean?"

"Just that you two have been out and about a lot since you and Jarod broke up. I saw you at the Rusty Nail the other night."

Texas shrugged. "We're just hanging out until he finds a new girlfriend soon."

The words left a bitter taste in her mouth, but it was only a matter of time before they were back to friends with zero benefits.

Harper nodded but didn't look convinced.

Will: *Bored.*

Texas: *No kidding. They talk in circles.*

She didn't have to listen to know half the town wanted the growth the expansion promised, including fast food chains and department stores. Others wanted to retain and promote the quaint, small town, rustic theme of family-owned shops and restaurants.

Will: *Help me stay awake.*

Texas: *JD's snoring will do that.*

She recognized the soft wheeze she'd come to love over the years as it competed with the arguing council. Will gave the older man a gentle nudge, and JD's snoring quieted.

Will drew his leg from the aisle and leaned forward, his elbows on his knees, head down, almost disappearing from view. Her phone signaled the arrival of a new text.

Will: *Send me a pic of your tits.*

She blinked at the explicit words. The heat in her face had just cooled, but now it flamed. Good thing she wore a leather vest over her T-shirt or anyone within six feet would have seen her nipples rise and pucker as if they preened for Will's attention. Shit. She hadn't expected him to continue sexting as part of the friends with benefits arrangement—a simple "hey, I'm horny" maybe. She certainly hadn't expected him to choose a time when she was cornered in a public place.

Yet, she couldn't deny the same lust enthralled her now as it had two nights ago. And she was stone cold sober this time. Her hands shook as she thumbed a reply.

Texas: *My breasts are not for your entertainment.*

Will: *IDK, I've entertained some damn naughty thoughts in the last 24 hours and most of them starred those pretty tits of yours.*

The traitorous "pretty tits" grew heavy, tingly, and ached for his mouth. Her chest tightened, and her breathing turned shallow and rapid.

Texas: *Tell me.*

God, she was insane, but anticipating his response made her heart pound.

Will: *I want to lick the valley between your tits, get them all wet, and squeeze them together.*

The taut cord from her breasts to her clit twanged like that of a guitar, and moisture pooled in her panties. She felt reckless, out of control…alive.

Texas: *More.*

Will: *Then I'll slide my dick through the silky vise.*

The throbbing in her pussy intensified. She straightened against the wall and pressed her thighs together, but the friction only increased her need. She swallowed a moan and gave him texted version to let him know she liked his fantasy.

Texas: *Mmmmmm.*

Will: *The head of my cock will tap your chin. You'll open for me and wet the tip with your tongue.*

Every nerve under her skin sizzled, and she struggled not to squirm. Her mind was fuzzy, making it difficult to form a response. Luckily, she didn't have to because he didn't wait for one.

Will: *Your nipples are plump little berries. I want you to pinch them while I fuck your tits.*

She sucked in a breath and blew it out.

Texas: *OMG, yes. I'm pinching them hard. I want to come.*

No lie there. One touch. That was all it would take.

Will: *You will. You'll scream my name. I'll fucking lose it and cum will shoot from my cock onto your throat.*

"Mmmahh." The sound erupted before she could hold it back.

"You okay? Harper asked.

Josh's gaze shifted from Will hunched over his phone to the one in her hand. A knowing smirk tilted his lips.

"I'm fine." She pressed the phone to her chest and scanned the room to see if anyone else had heard. If they hadn't, she was sure her face and body betrayed her sexually needy state just as easily.

Will was probably waiting for her to text him back. Another survey of the hall showed everyone's focus on the platform, except Jarod's. He was watching her, eyes narrowed as if he knew the dirty things Will said and her perverted reaction to them.

Shit. Her gaze dropped to her phone again. Big mistake.

Will: *I need to fuck you. Now.*

"Oh, my god," she muttered under her breath, both panic and lust wrangling for control. This was insane. She had to get out of here. She needed air.

Movement from her left had her head snapping up. Jarod had pushed off the wall and taken a step toward her. That was all she needed to get her feet moving. No way was she in the mood to deal with Jarod, and one word from Will and she'd jump his ass.

"Texas, we need—"

She flew out the door, into the thickly hot night air. The sun had gone down, and the cicadas were buzzing. Her boots tapped out a quick beat on the black paved lot as she headed for her truck. Yanking the fob out of her front pocket, she pressed the button. A few feet away, the taillights flashed from the darkened corner.

Two arms banded around her from behind, lifting her off her feet. Before she could scream, she was bent over the hood of her truck, the heavy weight of a man's body pinning her down, arms forced above her head. Panic gripped her throat with icy fingers.

"Jesus, T"—his breath fanned her cheek—"you don't know how bad my cock wants inside your hot, tight pussy."

Texas relaxed against the unforgiving metal, still warm from the scorching sun. "You scared the shit out of me."

"Sorry, but I'm so hard I could pound nails." Will ground his thick length into her ass, letting her feel exactly how hard he was.

She shuddered, his words along with the lasting effects of his texts overpowering her momentary fear. "What are you doing?"

"Shh." He nuzzled her neck as he transferred his hold so that both of her hands were imprisoned by one of his. The other smoothed its way down her arm and over her shoulder. It neared her underarm, and the fingers teased the side of her breast. "Just gotta check one thing."

His hand travelled farther south, over her hip and down her thigh. Her belly jerked when his fingers eased under the hem of her denim skirt and skimmed her inner thigh.

"Will, someone might see." Not that she cared with his thumb dipping under the elastic of her underwear. Hell, she actually sighed and spread her legs. Then the tip of one finger delved into her cunt, and she whimpered, aware of her arousal wetting his hand and her thigh.

"Ah, yeah, you like the idea of me fucking you over the hood of your truck. Don't you, baby?" He removed his finger and dragged one side of her panties down, down, down. The rest of the garment had no choice but to follow. When he'd tugged them as far as he could without releasing his hold on her hands, he let them fall around the top of her boots. With a little wiggle on her part, they dropped to her ankles.

He yanked at her skirt until the hem met her hips, and the air she'd thought of earlier as hot and thick now seemed cool compared to her body temperature. "Do you know how fucking sexy you are in this skirt?"

She hardly ever wore it, but something had made her drag it from the back of her closet for tonight. Probably some inner slut wanting exactly this to happen. Why couldn't it have told her to wear sexier undies? She stepped out of her white cotton panties and stretched her stance wider. God, she must have lost her mind, but she needed him to fulfill the fantasy he'd promised with his texts.

He shifted his hips to one side, and his palm covered one ass cheek. Still close to her ear, he whispered in a lust-thickened voice, "You walked in, those long legs stretching for miles, and all I could think about was how they'd feel around my hips, your calves squeezing my ass as my dick rocked your pussy."

The clang of his belt buckle and the whir of his zipper shimmied over her skin. Was she really doing this? Letting him fuck her over the hood of her truck in the parking lot of the town hall? Anyone could walk out and catch them. Plastic rattled and tore, and she pranced on tip-toes, her ass lifting and swaying like a mare eager for her stallion. Between his hands and the dirty talk, she was one hot mess and needy as all get out.

Hell, yeah, she was doing this.

"Damn." His frustration barely registered before she was suddenly lifted and swung in a one-eighty. The rear passenger door of his truck opened. "Get in."

On trembling legs, she hurled herself inside. He was right behind her. The door slammed, and the dome light went out. "What is it?"

Please don't tell me the condom is broken.

"Nothing. Come here."

She turned around, and her tummy did a somersault. He sat slumped against the door, his face framed in shadow, his shirt off—when had that happened?—and his jeans pushed to his knees. His cock stood tall and proud from a nest of dark curls and wrapped in latex. No holes to be seen.

A car engine roared across the lot, and headlights panned the darkened corner, then swung past them. Again, she questioned her sanity, but the danger of being caught only added to the thrill. She started to obey his command, but he issued another. "Take off your shirt and bra first."

Her gaze automatically flew to the cars

surrounding them. Not that she cared at this point.

"The meeting will go on for another hour at least." He hunkered lower, one long leg draped over the bench seat and the other foot planted in the floorboard. "Besides, I owe the city a street light."

She bent to look out the window and up at the street lamp. It was broken. "Did you do that?"

He grinned and shrugged. "I was hoping."

Texas shook her head, trying not to think about the fact he'd planned all this. Right now, nothing mattered but Will and the way he made her feel. Desirable. Wanted. And something she'd never let herself be — naughty.

With that thought, she gave him what she hoped was a sexy smile, stripped off her vest and T-shirt, and prayed the windows' dark tint took care of what he hadn't. Texas Tallulah Taylor was about to have sex in the backseat of a truck in the middle of the town hall parking lot.

****

Will's heart thumped against his chest at the smile Texas gifted him. Her lashes, painted black with mascara tonight, lowered to flushed cheeks, then lifted. Sultry eyes flashed a lusty green. Golden curls framed her face and tumbled around her shoulders. Damn, she was beautiful.

And he couldn't wait another minute to touch her. He crooked a finger at her and repeated, "Come here."

Texas climbed over his legs like some wild thing and straddled his hips. He gripped her waist over the wad of faded denim and settled her wet heat over his throbbing dick. He hissed in a breath at the sheer pleasure.

"Oh, sorry. I should take off my boots." She made as if to move, but he tightened his hold.

"Leave them on." He ran a hand down her silky thigh and over one knee until the tips of his fingers teased the skin just inside her boot. "I want to fuck you with your boots on."

Her eyes rounded then narrowed. "Whatever gets your kink on."

He smiled at her willingness to feed his fantasies. She'd surprised him more than once since the moment she admitted being turned on by that dickhead's texts. His little Tex was a sex kitten underneath all that no-nonsense business woman. But would she be so willing if he told her it was *her* and not the boots that got his kink on?

Instead, he reached for the front clasp of her bra. "I'll show you kink."

Milky white flesh spilled from the bra as the fastener popped, and he pushed the cups away. She arched her back, thrusting her tits higher, and the bra slid down her arms to the seat behind her. He sat up, eager for a taste of those sweet berries, but she shoved him back down and placed her hands over the twin globes. "You wanted to watch me play with my tits, right?"

Settling deeper against the door, Will swallowed and laid his hands to rest on her thighs. "It'd be my pleasure."

With a toss of her head, her hair floated down her back, allowing him a better view of her breasts or what he could see of them with her hands cupping the generous mounds. She lifted them and applied a light pressure then released them. They seemed to take on a life of their own, contracting, rising higher, the pink tips shrinking to hard buds.

His mouth watered. "I want to suck them."

"Uh-uh." She ran her thumbs over each nipple. Her head fell back, and the tip of her tongue slipped out to moisten her lips. He found himself mimicking her, licking his own lips in preparation for when she gave him the go ahead.

Then her thumb and finger bracketed the hard bud. With a twist, her nipple rolled, and a gasp escaped her parted lips. A squeeze and another roll, and she moaned. Her hips tilted, her pussy gliding forward over the length of his shaft. It jumped, trying to find entry. She rocked back, the downward slide drawing a groan from him.

Will dug his fingers into her thighs to keep from taking over. Watching Texas pleasure herself, taking pleasure from him, was intoxicating. He wanted to savor every moment. As much as he hoped his plan to make her fall in love with him worked, the possibility was there, in the back of his mind, that she wouldn't, and he needed this moment etched in his memory for when she called it quits.

He savored the slow, easy rhythm of her hips undulating, the grind of her pubic bone on his dick, her soaked curls tickling the sensitive ridge under the head, the way her ass mashed his balls on the down stroke. Her lip tucked between her teeth, the lusty sound of feminine desire that pried said lip loose. The freedom she allowed herself while under the influence of sexual pleasure. He absorbed every facet of the complex woman he loved.

The pace of her rocking increased. He wasn't sure how much longer he could last. "T, baby, you're killing me. Let me in."

Taking the slight nod as permission, Will grasped her hips, lifted, then lowered her onto his cock. He groaned as he slid into her welcoming heat. Every time with Texas felt like the first time and always better than the last. "Ride me, baby."

She picked up the steady rhythm, the slow roll of her hips reminding him of a night seven years ago when he'd watched her ride the mechanical bull at a bar in Austin. The wet dreams that vision had produced… Sweet Jesus, the real thing was so much better.

Each rotation dragged against his dick, soft on the forward motion, hard on the back. His breath rushed in and out, labored and heavy. The pressure in his balls grew, aching for release. No, not yet. He needed to touch her first, taste her, needed the moment to last longer. He had to take control before it was over and he was friend zoned again.

"Okay, my turn." Will let go of her hips, brushed her hands aside, and replaced them with his.

A soft murmur filled his ears and drifted over his damp skin. Her spine arched, filling his hands with supple flesh. He tested their weight, kneaded, then pinched the puckered tips. Her inner walls quivered around his cock. Oh, yeah, she liked that.

A trickle of sweat ran from his forehead along his jaw. Damn, it was hot in here, but he dare not stop to roll down the window. Instead, he repeated the action and tweaked the dark pink nipples. Her whole body jerked, and with a cry, she lost both her rhythm and her balance, arms flailing. One hand found the back of the passenger seat headrest, the other flattened against the steamed-fogged rear window.

"Again." Without waiting for him to comply, she rose on her knees. "Harder."

His gaze dropped to the gap she created between their bodies, and he groaned as she lowered again. Fuck, that was hot, watching the length of his shaft, glistening with her juices, swallowed by her glossy, pink pussy.

Another roll of her nipples sent her into a frenzied undulation of up, rock forward, down, slam home. "Oh, god, Will. Feels good."

The pattern was set, and damn, but he loved every minute. He ground his teeth against the urge to thrust upward on her downward plunge. Her hand on the back window made a loud squeak as it slipped. She slapped it back in place then higher, finding a dry spot without looking.

He smiled at what it must look like from the other side, with the window fogged up and a hand melting the steam away. And the truck had to be rocking. No doubt in anyone's mind what was happening inside. Especially with the noise she was making, that little engine purr.

"I'm close."

So was he. The base of his spine prickled, his balls drew tight, and his dick throbbed. He closed his eyes to shut out the erotic vision so he could hold off the inevitable, wanting to prolong the pleasure. Too fast. Too soon. But he couldn't deny her need to come.

He opened his eyes. "Let go, baby."

A sharp cry tore from her lips. Her cunt clamped around his cock, muscles rippling, sucking, demanding he follow her into heaven. And that's where she took him as cum shot through his shaft in hot, pulsing streams, pouring into the condom. He fought the instinct to close his eyes again and savor his release. How could he when the provocative image before him stole his breath.

It didn't matter. His vision clouded as the orgasm overwhelmed him. A groan forced its way past his throat as searing pleasure pulsed in waves like those made by a pebble hitting the surface of a still pond, rolling on and on. So good. So fucking good.

Texas slumped forward, forcing him to catch her. He lowered her to lie against his chest, their slick bodies slipping and sliding. Her breath came in quick, short puffs that tickled his neck. He let his hands roam her shoulders, back, and hips, lightly tracing her curves. Drinking in the silky texture of her smooth skin, he let himself believe they would share moments like this in the future, that he could have her this way forever.

"I can't move." Her voice sounded as dreamy as he felt.

"Me either." He could, but he didn't want to.

"I suppose we have to." She didn't budge.

"Maybe in a minute."

Neither moved except for the lazy treks of his fingers along her back. The sound of cicadas invaded the quiet of the cab. Somewhere in the distance a cat yowled. Sweat pooled between their bellies, and he caught a drop that ran from her neck down her spine.

Her muscles tensed, and a second later, she pushed up to allow a couple inches between them. "We're going to melt if we don't get up."

She grappled for leverage and sat up before he could convince her they wouldn't melt, that he didn't mind the sweltering heat. Liked it, even. Instead, he reached between them and grabbed the base of his cock to hold the condom on as she lifted off him and crawled backward to flop onto the seat.

"You bought new floor mats."

The random comment let him know their moment of intimacy was over, and she'd compartmentalized their relationship back to friendship. Probably for the best. As part of his altered plan to keep her guard down so he could work his way into her heart without her realizing it, he'd decided to get her to spend some time with him doing something other than having sex.

Sighing, he sat forward, popped the console between the front seats, and felt around for one of the fast food napkins he kept stashed there. The hard industrial plastic mats under his feet were new, made to protect the carpet, and easy to wash down—good for ranch life—but they were the last thing he wanted to think about. "Yeah, a couple of months ago."

"I like 'em." She turned in the seat, first one way, then the other, and came up with her bra. "Might have to get some."

He grunted, wadded the condom in the napkin, and stuffed it in the cup holder to throw away later. By the time he hitched up his underwear and jeans and buckled his belt, she had her skirt pulled down and her bra fastened. He found his shirt and tucked his head and arms through the holes as she yanked hers over her breasts and down to the waist of her skirt.

Friend. Friend. Be her goddamned friend.

Will opened the door and stepped down on the hard pavement. A splotch of white near her front tire drew his attention. Her panties. He'd completely forgotten about them in his hurry to get her in the truck when a car started across the lot.

Swiping them up, he tossed them to her. "What happened to the hot pink ones?"

A gasp hissed at him as she snatched them against her stomach. Even with the harsh glare of the dome light, her flushed cheeks gave away her embarrassment. She balled the undergarment in her fist and scooched to the edge of the seat, then slid to the ground. "Ass."

She veered around him in a fake huff, and he chuckled as he shut the door to his truck and turned to watch her slide behind the wheel of hers. He stepped in the way before she could close the door and leaned an arm on the roof. "Got plans tomorrow?"

"Why? You want to take an inventory of my underwear?"

He laughed, though the idea made his dick twitch. Then he could imagine stripping her of different colors as he— No, can't think about that right now or he'd have her naked again in the front seat of *her* pickup. "Talking about it the other night got me to thinking how long it's been since I've been to the lake for more than just to clean up or mow around the buildings out there. I thought we might go for a swim, like old times."

"Sounds nice." She stuck the key in the ignition and started the engine. "I wish I could, but the roofer is coming to patch the north corner of the house. His earlier repairs didn't work, and the rain last week left a puddle in my washroom."

"Why didn't you say something? I could have sent a couple of the guys to take care of it." Why he asked, he didn't know. She was stubborn about taking care of herself to the point she'd rather suffer than ask for help.

"They have their own job to do, and the roofer guaranteed his work, so it's not costing me anything to have him do it." She sat back and tugged the seatbelt across her chest. The strap divided her breasts and made him want to— "How about Wednesday?"

He backed out of the door and shut it, hoping the physical barrier would be enough. Though once he put his brain to work to answer her question, his stirring erection withered. "Can't. I'll be in Houston."

"Oh." Her brows dove into a V, and her green eyes searched his face. "Want some company for the drive?"

"Nah, I'm good." And he sure as hell didn't want her to know why he was going.

"How about Thursday?"

"I might not be back. How about Friday?"

She bit her lip, and he was sure she'd say no. Friday was one of the busiest days at the barn. Then her lips quirked upward as if she wanted to smile for his sake but couldn't muster the emotion behind it. Something was swirling in that head of hers. "Sure. Can't stay all day, but I can come out for a while."

His gut relaxed. The fact her answer meant so much wasn't lost on him. And it wasn't something new. The need to see her, touch her, even just breathe the same air as Texas was a constant ache he'd lived with for years and became increasingly harder to live without.

"Will?" She latched onto his arm through the window, her expression etched with worry. "You're not sick, are you? Is that why you're going to Houston and don't want me along? Are you having tests?"

Shit. He should have known what she'd be thinking. He laid a hand on hers. "No, T. I'm not sick, so get the notion out of your head."

Relief softened her features, and she nodded, blinking her moist eyes dry.

"Hey, I promised you'd be the first to know if something like that ever came up, right?"

"I know. I just…" She swallowed.

"I know." Tempted to haul her through the window and into his arms, he slapped a palm on the roof of her truck and backed away. "See you Friday."

She still didn't look convinced but shifted into reverse and glanced behind her. "Yep."

Propping his ass against the front fender of his pickup, he taunted, "I'll ice down a watermelon, and we'll have a seed spitting contest."

As he'd hoped, the smile she flashed reached her eyes. "Won't do any good. I'm still the champ."

Will watched Texas exit the parking lot, then climbed into his truck and headed home. Alone.

It was getting harder and harder to face an empty house, to sleep in an empty bed, to be away from her at all. Four days felt like forever from now. And the hands-off afternoon at the lake to show her he wanted more than just sex from her sounded damn near impossible. Especially with it being so far away. And with the reason for his trip to Houston weighing on him.

Four days. Four damn long, lonely days.

Chapter Five

The roof was fixed, "guaranteed" this time. Or was that *again*? And the activity in and around the house had occupied Texas and kept her thoughts off Will. Mostly.

However, it was late Wednesday afternoon, and no amount of paperwork or questions from staff could take her mind off him and the sudden trip to Houston. She believed him when he said he was okay, but something about the way he'd averted his gaze and avoided telling her why he was going didn't sit right. She'd given him several openings to tell her, but he obviously hadn't wanted her to know.

She'd tossed and turned all night, running different scenarios, trying to reason through his silence. Will hated the city. He sent his foreman when he could. When he couldn't, Will took care of business and got the hell out. He never spent the night. Whatever called him there had to be important.

Or whoever.

The band around her chest tightened and her stomach rolled as the little voice in her head twisted the knife. The only reason she'd come up with as to why he wouldn't volunteer the information ate at her. Another woman.

She dropped her pen on the clipboard, the inventory of supplies to order a blur of disinterest, and mashed the heels of her hands against her eyes. The black spots from the pressure didn't erase the images of hotel sheets and the erotic dance of two naked bodies—sleek golden legs entwined with lean muscular ones, trim hips undulating, feminine sighs, his face buried in long dark hair, that whiskey deep voice whispering dirty words in her ear.

Texas swallowed the lump in her throat and slammed her palms on the desk. She refused to acknowledge the emotions swirling inside her. They were only friends. Will was a man. And really, it was his MO. He grew bored, restless, never staying with one woman very long. She just never thought she'd be one of those women.

And if she really thought about it, he'd been a little less enthusiastic last night. Sure, he'd started out as ready for action as the night at her place, instigating a round of sexting that had them both horny and then attacking her in the parking lot. The memory of having his hard body pressing her over the hood of her truck sent a zing of tingling sensation straight to her clit.

But then he'd let her take control and something in his demeanor changed. He'd barely said a word, the exciting, naughty talk silenced as if he'd lost interest or gone somewhere else in his head. Not that the sex hadn't been good. Just thinking about how hard she'd come made her face hot, her tummy flutter, and her panties wet.

And speaking of panties, the way he'd thrown her plain white undies at her...

Hot pink lace? Who was she kidding? She was only playing dress up, and no amount of sexy lingerie would make a difference. She wasn't his type at all. He liked women who glittered — sequins, bangles, hell, even their makeup sparkled. And she was a white cotton panty girl.

But she'd known that for years. So why did she suddenly ache to be more, to be like those other women?

A clickety-clack echoed down the hall, getting louder and more annoying until it stopped outside her office. The door opened, and Krystal Whitaker breezed in on four-inch heels and wearing a white halter dress that showed off more golden skin than should be legal. "Where's Will?"

"How should I know?" Texas usually pretended civility for Will's sake, but she couldn't muster the patience today. Maybe because Krystal was a reminder of all she would never be.

Krystal dropped the largest handbag Texas had ever seen on the desk, dragged a metal chair from the corner, and folded her model-thin frame into it. "Because he tells you everything."

Not everything. "Well, he's not here."

"Look, I know you don't like me." She crossed her slender legs and adjusted the bracelets around one boney wrist. "I don't like you either, but for some reason, Will does. So can we just skip to the part where you tell me what I need to know, and I'll get out of your hair?"

Texas sighed. Will's whereabouts weren't a secret. What he was doing was another story. "He's in Houston."

Perfectly dark brows arched high on a smooth forehead. "What's he doing there?"

The band around her chest squeezed another notch tighter. "Don't have a clue."

"Hmph." Krystal's frown deepened. "When will he be back?"

"Thursday is all I know."

"It's not like him to be so secretive."

No, it wasn't, but she didn't like that the woman who'd cheated on Will now tried to find fault with him. "He's not. He just didn't say, and I didn't ask." Not straight out, anyway.

Krystal must have decided Texas had little else to offer because she rose from the chair and looped the handle of her purse over one shoulder. "If he calls you, please tell him I need to talk to him."

"Sure." Though he probably wouldn't call. He hadn't done more than text last night to ask if the roof was fixed and again this morning to say he was heading out. She'd texted back for him to let her know he made it safely, but he hadn't replied, and he should have been there hours ago.

Krystal started to turn away then hesitated. Red lips that had formed a tight line softened. The frown on her perfectly made up face shifted from annoyed to uncertain. "Texas, please. I really need to talk to him. It's important."

The fact the woman said please and the quiet desperation in her voice made Texas blink. She almost felt sorry for her. Almost. "I'll tell him."

"Thank you." The acknowledgment of gratitude was followed by the lift of her chin as the mask of superiority fell back into place. Without another word, she swished her way out of the office, not bothering to close the door behind her.

"That was weird." And more than a little awkward.

Only one bit of relief had come from the visit. Whatever reason sent Will to Houston, whether he was with another woman or not, it wasn't Krystal.

****

Will stood as the only woman he'd ever loved besides Texas entered the hotel bar. Three years older than the last time he'd seen her and a little too thin, Melissa Renee Sanderson was still a beautiful woman. Dark brown hair cut chin length, sun-kissed skin that would have been perfect if not for the overuse of makeup, and the trademark glossy pink nails she was never without. His mother took care of herself, and he had the receipts to prove it.

"Don't you look handsome." She slid a hand over the lapel of his jacket, fingering the material. "Armani?"

"No." It was the same suit he'd worn the day he buried his father. She'd have known that if she'd bothered to show up for the funeral. Instead, she'd called a week later to find out if the will had been read and what Charlie might have left her. Somehow, it seemed appropriate to wear the damn suit today.

"Hmm, I see the lack of quality now." She tilted

her face toward him.

"Missy." He bent to air kiss the proffered cheek. God forbid he actually touched her or called her mother.

"Are we dining?" She smoothed the side of her hair as if he'd mussed it. "I'm starved."

"Our reservation was for two hours ago." He'd given up and waited in the bar, knowing she'd show up when she was good and ready. Missy, as she preferred he call her, never adjusted to anyone's schedule.

"I'm sure they'll have a table." Not waiting for his reply, she breezed through the bar and out the door.

Will had no choice but to follow across the lobby to the restaurant. Not if he wanted this business with her done. Her late arrival had given him plenty of time to rehearse his speech, yet the moment he saw her again, he couldn't ignore that little place inside him that ached for her to change, to be the mother he never had.

One smile at the young maître de of the restaurant, and his mother had him fawning over her and ushering them to an empty table.

"How are things in Nowheresville?" She slid into the chair he pulled out. "I'll bet nothing's changed."

"Not much." He didn't bother to expand as he sat across from her. She wasn't really interested anyway.

She smiled knowingly. "So, you're still hung up on Texas?"

Somehow, his mother had figured out his feelings for Texas. He'd called it maternal instinct until he realized her only instinct was finding a person's weaknesses so she could exploit them. "She's not up for discussion."

"Very well then, what shall we talk about?" She draped her napkin over her lap. "Oh, I know. You should see Paris this time of year. Simply gorgeous. I really hated to leave."

"Why did you?"

The peevish look she gave him would have flooded him with guilt ten years ago, maybe even as recent as five. Now, it only confirmed his need to be done with her.

"I told you why." She opened her menu, held it out farther, and peered down her nose at the options. Her conceit wouldn't allow for reading glasses.

"Your latest, Lars Rezensky, was it? He dumped you, right?"

"Don't be rude." She folded the menu and laid it to one side. "Actually, his daughter didn't approve of our relationship. Yes, he did tell me it was over, but I know that bitch was behind his decision."

"So what are your plans now?" The question could have waited until after dinner, but his stomach might as well have been filled with lead.

"I'm entertaining several options." She tilted her head, and her lips turned up in a half smile meant to disarm him. "I could stay here for a while or out at the ranch."

The thought that she'd stay never crossed his

mind. Ranch life hadn't suited her before. Why should it now? She only threw the possibility out there to lure him in, make him hope she'd ever want that life. It didn't work. Even if she truly changed her mind, he wanted no part of her, not anymore.

From the moment he'd learned Texas refused Jarod's proposal, Will knew he had to stop trying not to love her. That would never happen, and frankly, it hurt too much to try. On the other hand, holding on to a child's love for his mother when there was nothing left was equally as difficult. When his mother had called to say she'd be passing through Houston on her way to wherever, he'd made up his mind to cut the cord. Permanently. As much as he wanted Texas in his life, he realized he wanted—needed—his mother out of it.

If not for his sake, then for the sake of any future he hoped to have with Texas.

"I also have an invitation to join a friend in Monte Carlo." *Here it comes.* "I had hoped you'd help me out."

He didn't hesitate. "How much help do you need?"

Her smile brightened. It always did when she got her way. "Twenty-five thousand should set me nicely for a while."

Will ignored the vibration of his phone—probably another text from Texas—and dipped into the coat pocket for the check folded beside it. Opening the check up, he laid it on the table, pressed his fingers on the top edge, and slid it across the table.

Missy didn't lean forward, though her body tensed as if she wanted to. Her eyes rounded, and she glanced up at him then back at the check with five zeroes between the first number and the decimal point. His money was mostly tied up in property and stock, but he'd liquidated a few investments, which had put his broker in a tailspin, and sold a few head of cattle, including his prize bull. It was worth the loss to put this offer, literally, on the table.

She reached for the check, but when her fingers closed around one corner, he applied enough pressure to hold it in place. Her gaze flew to his in question.

"This is it," he said. "The last of it."

"I don't understand."

"No." He shook his head. "You don't. You never have and you never will."

"Fine, keep your damn money." She sat back in her chair, trying to pretend the money meant nothing to her, but she couldn't quite pull it off. Greed overrode indifference.

"Dad would roll over in his grave if he knew I'd given you a dime. He worked his ass off for it. So have I." He leaned forward. "If you take this check, spend it wisely, because it's the last penny you'll ever get from me. I want you out of my life."

"You don't mean that."

"I do." He withdrew his hold on the check, leaving it out there in the middle of the table between the salt and pepper and the retro centerpiece made of chrome. He hadn't intended to give her the option, but it was one final test. One he knew she'd fail. Hoped she'd fail.

She lifted her chin and picked up the check. "I gave up my best years on that godforsaken ranch. I deserve this."

Will stood and looked down at the woman he'd wasted his whole life trying to please. She didn't know how to give, only take and take until there was nothing left. In that moment, he realized how much the other women in his life resembled her—high maintenance, selfish, manipulative. The exact opposite of Texas. Maybe that's why he loved her so much and why he could never love them.

He smiled at his own foolishness and tipped an imaginary hat. "Have a nice life, *Mother*."

Walking away should have felt wrong or sad. Instead, he just felt dirty. And in need of a drink. He headed straight back to the bar and settled on the same stool he'd vacated earlier. Waiting for his mother, he'd kept to soda so he'd have a clear head, but now...

He looked at the bartender. "Whiskey."

The phone in his pocket vibrated again. He took it out and read the texts, all from Texas.

From early this morning.

T: *Text me to let me know you made it safely.*

The next came at two fifty-three.

T: *You there yet?*

An hour ago.

T: *Hello?*

The one he'd ignored moments ago.

T: *Don't make me come find you.*

And the last.

T: *Are you okay?*

He should have answered her by now. And he should have told her what he was doing. But she would have insisted on coming with him. He didn't want her involved, didn't want any of the dirt rubbing off on her, the only honest and real thing in his life.

Will punched in a message.

Will: *I'm fine. Talk to you tomorrow.*

The bartender set the shot of whiskey in front of him. He slugged it back and motioned for another.

Part of him wished he'd have let Texas come with him. Damn, but he'd welcome the comfort of her arms. A shudder racked his body. He'd be dick-deep in her sweet heat and losing himself, washing away the blackness surrounding his soul. The whiskey would have to do.

With a heavy sigh, he downed the amber liquor. He glanced up at the bartender. "Keep 'em comin'."

Chapter Six

The sun beat down, the glare of its reflection bouncing off the water and blinding Texas through closed lids. The afternoon had been exactly as Will promised. Like old times. Fun, sun, laughter, and the freedom from the stress of adult life.

She'd arrived around noon, not quite sure what to expect. The lack of communication on Wednesday and the lack of a promised call on Thursday had her cagey. But he'd put her at ease with a familiar grin and waited long enough for her to shed the T-shirt and cutoffs she wore over her bikini before he shoved her off the edge of the deck. After that, they swam to the buoy, played king of the inner tube, and fought over the last pickle. He hadn't touched her the entire day except to dunk her or push her in.

And all she'd thought about was how hot he looked with his bathing suit riding low, showing off the V carved from hipbones to groin. The way water dripped from his hair and ran in rivulets down the sleek bronzed muscles of his chest. She'd sucked in more lake water today than from the collective days of their childhood. How was she supposed to concentrate on staying afloat with the way his hands felt on her skin, even with the most innocent touch?

She lay beside him on a beach towel, the hard

planks of the deck resistant and unforgiving under her not so young body and more than the sun making her hot. She ached to simply roll over and plant one on him.

Think about something else. Tell him about your visit from Krystal.

Her mouth opened, but she couldn't force the words past her lips. She didn't want to ruin the moment by bringing up his ex. This day was theirs, just two old friends getting back to old times.

Texas sensed Will's movement as he rolled toward her, his long, lean body only inches from hers. He must have propped his head in his hand because the brightness of the sun disappeared and his shadow offered cool relief to her face. Her heartbeat tripled. She waited for him to speak, but he remained quiet. Her imagination conjured images of him scanning her body with those dark and hungry eyes.

Was he thinking about kissing her? All he had to do was tip forward —

Friends, remember? With a mental shake of her head, she tried to clear the erotic thoughts. *Really, Texas, he's probably more interested in the scenery.*

Either way, his silence made her nervous. "Can you be a little quieter? I can hear your gears turning."

He grunted, but she heard the smile behind it. Another minute of crickets passed before he finally spoke. "Get to know you?"

Texas smiled, memories flooding her thoughts. It had been years since either of them had said those words. Get To Know You was the game they'd played the day they met. He'd said his dad invented the game when Will first went to kindergarten. He'd been scared, afraid he wouldn't know anyone, wouldn't have any friends. His dad told him all he had to do was ask a question, then another, and he'd have a friend in no time. She and Will played it all the time as kids until they knew everything there was to know about each other, then later as teens when they needed to talk about touchy subjects. As adults they'd stopped playing games and simply asked what they wanted to know.

She shrugged. "What do you want to know?"

"Why didn't you say yes?"

"You'll have to be a little more specific than that."

"To Jarod, when he proposed."

She'd wondered when he'd get around to asking about the reason for her break up with Jarod. She hadn't told him about the proposal, just told him they'd parted ways. That he somehow knew shouldn't have surprised her either. Theirs was a small town. "I don't know. I could have. He's a great guy. Makes good money, doesn't drink or do drugs, he's kind, thoughtful, and on and on. I know he loves me. I might have learned to love him."

"But?"

"Don't get me wrong. I care about him. But there was just no…passion." She opened her eyes and rolled her head to look at him. "I couldn't make myself settle for less. It wouldn't have been fair to either of us."

But you'll settle for what little Will offers?

Was that what she was doing? Taking scraps, pretending he thought of her the same as the asshole sending her texts thought about his lover? No, this was different. Will wasn't settling down material. She knew that up front. She didn't expect more than a few weeks of sex before the new wore off and he moved on. No strings. Fun sex. That was it.

Then why did the mere thought of him with someone else make her stomach turn, her chest constrict, and moisture burn the back of her eyelids? The little sleep she'd gotten in the past two nights were filled with dreams of her standing beside the bed in a hotel room, watching him make love to some faceless woman.

Just ask him.

"So, um, how was your trip?"

The thoughtful light in his eyes went cold. He looked away as he rolled to his back and put an arm over his forehead. "Fine."

The knot in her stomach tightened a few degrees. "Doesn't sound fine."

He heaved in a deep breath and let it out. "My mom was passing through Houston and wanted to see me."

A warm rush of relief battled icy fingers of dread. When Will was a boy, before his mother walked out on him and his father, she'd used him as a weapon against his dad, threatening to take him away. As Will grew up, she'd used him for an emotional crutch when her crummy life fell apart, which was often. And since his dad passed and Will controlled the purse strings, she pretty much gave up pretending any maternal connection. Communication became more infrequent and only when her bank account ran dry.

Texas searched his face, but he hid his feelings well. "What did she want this time?"

"Same as usual. Her latest boyfriend dumped her, and she needed money to get to some other guy in Monte Carlo."

"Oh, Will." She sat up to lean on one palm, though she itched to touch him, to offer comfort. "Why didn't you tell me? I could have been there with you." She'd been the buffer between him and his bitch of a mother more times than she could count. The woman never failed to make him feel like a means to an end, that his only worth was what she could get out of him.

"I didn't want to put you through the drama."

"Would have been better than what I was thinking." She almost choked on the muttered admission as it slipped from her mouth, and she rushed to cover the mistake. "I'm sorry. I know how much she can still hurt you."

"It's gotten easier. I give her money to get rid of her. It works. I don't think I'll see her again."

Until next time. There was always a next time with Missy Sanderson. Enough was never enough. Texas tried to be sensitive to Will's feelings, but god, she hated that woman.

"So?" Eyes still closed, brows already furrowed against the sun, his frown deepened. "What were you thinking that could be worse than my mother? I already told you I wasn't sick."

Shit. "Nothing." Her cheeks flushed with the lie, hotter than the sunburn she'd regret later. Thank god, he couldn't see it.

"I can tell you're lying. I can hear it in your voice." His long lashes lifted to reveal a sliver of coffee-brown eyes. "Spit it out."

Texas swiveled forward to rest on both hands behind her, wishing he didn't know her quite so well. She lifted a shoulder and let it drop. "I thought maybe you might have been meeting someone."

"Someone?" The wheels in his head were spinning now, and he obviously didn't like where they were leading. She knew him as well as he knew her. "As in a woman?"

"Yeah. I mean, you don't go into the city if you can help it. You hate it, and here you were, spending the night." She shrugged again, hoping he'd take it as indifference. "And you didn't act like you wanted to tell me why you were going, which you would have done if it was business, so…"

His arm lifted off his forehead, and his head craned off the deck. "Jesus, Texas. Did you really think I'd fuck you in the back seat of my truck one night, all the time planning a hook up with someone else the next?" He sat up, making a snorting sound as he reached for his T-shirt. "You don't think very much of me, do you?"

"It's not that." She straightened and drew her arms around bent knees, not sure if she'd hurt his feelings or his pride. "We said no strings. And you said we could walk away if we met someone."

"If I'd met someone, you'd know." He shoved his head through the shirt, then his arms, the material complaining at the seams. When the shirt hid the rippling muscles of his back and settled around his waist, he turned to look at her for a long moment, a storm of emotion swirling in his eyes, then he shook his head and looked away. "You of all people should know how I feel about cheating. I'd never do that."

"But that's just it." She reached for her T-shirt and shorts, feeling small and naked in the shadow of his disappointment. And maybe a little defensive. "It wouldn't be cheating. We aren't in a relationship. Just…friends with benefits."

His gaze sliced over her, and his jaw worked as if he wanted to argue. But his silence said what he didn't.

She stood and slipped the shirt over her head to hide the tears that snuck up on her. Where the hell was all this hurt coming from? Stepping into her shorts, she searched for her keys.

"Are you leaving?"

"Yeah, it's getting late." Where were her damn keys?

There, by the cooler. She had to step over his legs to get to them. He grabbed her hand, stopping her. "Don't go. Not like this. I'm sorry."

A lump built in her throat as she tugged free. What the hell was wrong with her? "It's fine. We're good. I shouldn't have stayed so long, and tomorrow'll be a hard day." Swiping up her keys, she waved in the direction of the food and slid into her flip-flops. "Take this home so you won't have to cook tonight. I'll pick up the cooler next time I'm out."

"I'll bring it to the barn tomorrow."

She felt him rise behind her. Part of her wanted him to reach for her, to take her in his arms and tell her everything would be okay. The other part of her wanted to run like hell before whatever this was burning in her chest broke free. "Sounds good."

Forcing the most sincere smile she could muster, she turned around and ruffled the top of his sun-streaked hair. "I had fun today. We should do this more often."

He didn't bother to return the smile but nodded. "We will."

If only she could be as sure as he sounded. "See ya later?"

"Yeah." He backed up to let her pass.

The gesture felt like a clear invitation to leave, and she didn't wait for the old heave-ho. Her legs shook as she strode up the long pier, her worst nightmare coming true. Less than a week and things between them were unraveling. At this rate, how much longer could their friendship survive?

****

Will sat in his truck, once again staring at the dim light streaming from her bedroom window. Every instinct told him to walk right inside and tell Texas he loved her. She was still awake. He'd seen her shadow pass across the wall minutes ago. That was why he was here, wasn't it? To spill his guts and hope for the best. Fuck his plan.

Yet, he couldn't get his head around all the questions and uncertainty their argument left him with. Damn, he was having a hard time reading her these days.

He closed his eyes, and the clear picture of her meadow-green ones, wounded and misting with tears she tried to hide, filled his mind. What he couldn't be sure of was what upset her. The thought of him with someone else or his anger?

He shouldn't have lost his temper. But damn it all, he'd still been suffering from the biggest hangover since leaving his teens. After returning home from his trip, he'd spent the rest of the day popping pain relievers and trying to sweat the alcohol from his system. He'd fallen into bed early and still wasn't himself when he went to meet Texas at the lake.

Add to everything else the frustration of having to see her in the skimpy little bikini that bared more of her silky flesh than he could resist. He'd had to sneak a touch here and there under the guise of acting a fool.

But watching her walk away had cleared his head like nothing else, and he wouldn't sleep tonight if he didn't make things right. If only he knew how.

Well, it won't get done if you don't get off your ass.

Hoping he'd figure out something before she answered the door, he climbed out of his truck, grabbed the cooler from the back, and headed up the front walk. Through the glass pane in the door, a light shone from the kitchen. He lightly rapped his knuckles on the smooth wood.

A turbaned head poked around the kitchen doorway, her surprise then recognition easy to read. And the hesitation on her face was hard to miss. Yep, he'd screwed up.

Her actions were slow, almost reluctant, as she pulled the towel from her head on the way to the door. Hair damp, long pale legs bare, she wore the same nightshirt he'd caught her in before, and damn if his cock didn't make a slow stretch toward the waist of his jeans, despite the gnawing in his gut. Jacking off in the shower before coming over, hoping it would offer some control, had been a waste of time.

The door opened, and Texas leaned against it, looking at him, the ends of her hair caught between two handfuls of towel in an effort to dry them. Up close, the wets spots her hair left on her shirt might as well have been glass as transparent as they were. The pink circles around her nipples stood out like targets.

"You didn't have to bring it tonight."

It took him a moment to figure out what she was talking about, then he remembered the cooler in his hand. "I know." He lifted his gaze to meet hers. "I couldn't leave things like that between us...I'm sorry."

She smiled, and it reached her eyes, along with something else he couldn't quite read. Relief maybe. "Me, too."

"We should talk."

"Yeah." The gap in the door widened as she

stepped back. "You want coffee?"

"Sure."

"You can leave that outside." She waved one hand at the cooler and turned away. "I'll be right back."

Will set the ice chest on the porch, started forward, then halted. Arms stretched over her head gathering her hair, she walked up the stairs, the hem of her nightshirt teasing the underside of her ass. White cotton panties flirted with the raging hard-on behind his fly, and that was all it took clear his head.

"You know where everything's at," she called over her shoulder. "Help yourself."

A grin split his face, all confusion and indecision shoved to the wayside. Hell if he wasn't sticking with what he knew. "That's an invitation I won't refuse."

Chapter Seven

The front door slammed, and Texas stopped at the top of the stairs. Was he leaving?

She turned to find Will right behind her. "What—"

He plowed into her, driving her backward, his hands framing her face. Her back hit the wall outside her bedroom as his head lowered. His lips slanted over hers in a kiss that zinged all the way to her toes, then shot straight to her core. This wasn't supposed to happen again. The feelings she'd struggled with all afternoon scared the hell out of her, and she'd made up her mind to end this game they were playing before someone got hurt. Before *she* got hurt.

But Will made it impossible to think.

The hard length of his body pinned her to the faded wallpaper. His tongue painted the inside of her mouth in heated strokes. He shoved one knee between her legs, lifting her higher, and ground his hips into hers. Her head spun as his thick denim-covered cock rocked her clit. Oh, god.

He tore his mouth from hers in a groan and rested his forehead against the side of her head. His ragged breath near her ear made her shiver.

She clutched his shirt. "I thought you wanted to

talk."

"I do." His lips brushed her temple, and his hand fell away from her face to land on her thigh. "We will." He curled his fingers around the back of her knee and drew her leg higher, hooking it over his hip. His big hand skimmed her thigh and dove under her underwear to cup her ass. "Later."

"Will, this—"

A rotation of his pelvis splintered the edges of her world, tiny shards of ecstasy trying to find their way to the center, but then it receded as he relieved the pressure, leaving her wanting more.

"I need you, T." His lips feathered along her jaw. Long fingers traced the seam of her ass. "Please, don't say no. Don't make me stop."

The sexy rasp of his voice would have demolished her willpower if she'd had any. "No, I won't."

With a grunt of approval and one hand on her ass, the other around at the back of her neck, he swung her away from the wall. She wrapped her other leg around him and locked her ankles at the base of his spine as he carried her into the bedroom. At her bed, he stopped, but he didn't let her go. Instead, he kissed her again, the same hungry taking of her lips.

Texas tugged at his shirt, trying to find the hem so she could feel the heat of his skin, but it was trapped under her calves. She whimpered and let her legs drop until her feet touched hard wood. Obviously, Will had the same idea because he grabbed a fistful of her shirt and yanked it upward.

She had to let go of him, and their mouths parted, so he could get it over her head and arms. His shirt followed hers to the floor. She reached for her panties.

"Let me." He fell to his knees, both hands bracketing her hips. Soft open-mouthed kisses dotted her belly above the elastic.

Her stomach muscles jerked, but she couldn't enjoy it for the embarrassment of being caught once again in plain white cotton. "Next time, give me a little warning so I can put on something sexier."

Next time? What was she thinking? There couldn't be a next time.

Dark lashes lifted, and the fire in his eyes as he peered up at her from beneath them ended all arguments with herself about this time, next time, or any other time.

"Are you kidding?" He ran his thumbs along the edge of elastic around her hips. "I love these. They're sexy in their own way. They're very Texas. Soft and feminine." His tongue dipped into her bellybutton. "Clean. Fresh. Innocent." His fingers breached the waistband at the top of her buttocks and dragged her underwear down a fraction, knuckles grazing her cheeks, then hips as they slid to the front, still tucked beneath the briefs. "Pure and sweet."

She would have snorted if his thumbs hadn't finally met at the top of her mound and if he hadn't nipped at the cotton-covered folds below them. Her breath hitched, and her fingers sifted through his golden-brown hair. She wanted to pull him closer, but the anticipation of not knowing his next move was more potent. "I thought you liked dirty."

He smiled that sexy smile, the one that made her knees weak. "I like both, especially on you."

Another bite, harder this time, teeth mashing the material against her clit. A moan escaped her throat, and her fingers curled into fists around the soft waves. Moisture seeped from her pussy to saturate an already damp crotch.

"Besides, warning you would take away the element of surprise, wouldn't it?" He lowered her panties an inch to reveal the top of her folds.

"Yes."

His thumbs played over the flesh still covered, back and forth. "That wouldn't be as exciting, would it?"

She tilted her hips, seeking relief yet not wanting the teasing to end. "No."

"And see how wet you are, how excited?" His tongue dipped into the small crevice above her panties.

A small shock of pleasure streaked through her. "Yes."

The material lowered another inch. His tongue speared deeper between her folds, stabbing at her clit. The shock became a jolt of lightning. Heat licked at every nerve ending. "Oh, god, Will. Stop."

He drew back.

"No, don't stop." She tried to pull his mouth back to her pussy. "Just quit torturing me."

With a chuckle, he lowered her panties all the way to her feet. She stepped out of them and spread her legs. But he only laughed again, rose to his feet, and unbuttoned his fly. "Get on the bed."

"Let me help you." She reached for his zipper, but he caught her wrists.

"No." He walked her backward two steps until her knees hit the mattress. His gaze locked on hers. "I'm about to explode. I want to be inside you when I do."

Her tummy quivered, not only from his words or the thought of his cock buried deep inside her, but from the hungry and almost pained look in his eyes. He wanted her. He wanted Texas Tallulah Taylor. He'd said so before, even shown her. But tonight, she really understood and believed.

As she scooted to the middle of the bed and watched him shuck his boots, socks, jeans and briefs in seconds flat, then stalk toward her, she marveled at the fact that Will—her Will, her best friend—found *her*—plain white cotton panty Texas—sexy and he wanted her. The idea did funny things to her insides, making them soft and squishy.

He crawled up her body, forcing her to drop from her elbows to her back. Before her head hit the mattress, his lips meshed with hers. Tongue swirled around tongue. Skin sizzled over skin. Her legs opened, and his hip settled between them. His hands roamed every inch of her body—knees, thighs, waist, breasts, arms. Then he laced his fingers with hers and held them beside her head.

The broad head of his cock rested at her opening. She lifted her hips, inviting. With a growl, he flexed his hips and thrust.

He swallowed her cry and thrust again, his wide girth stretching her, filling her. She dug her heels into the bed for leverage and arched into his next lunge. He groaned, and she drank it in. Then his tongue and cock began a leisurely pace of in and out. Pressure built deep in her core, but held steady.

Texas sensed rather than felt the shift in Will, an internal stillness. He didn't stop the gentle gyration of his hips, but his mouth left hers to trail along her jaw.

"You feel so good." His words whispered against the sensitive spot below her ear. "I…"

She opened her eyes as he lifted his head. The tenderness reflected in the dark depth of his chocolate gaze stirred up all the emotion she'd fought that afternoon. Her chest constricted, the band around it tightening. The longer she looked into his eyes, the higher and stronger it became until it nearly overwhelmed her. And yet she couldn't look away.

The room closed in on them, smaller and smaller, its black edges surrounding them. The sound of their labored breathing and the beat of her heart echoed in the confined space. Moisture burned the back of her eyelids. She turned her head to one side and bit her lip to ward off the tears.

"Shh, it's okay." He kissed her cheek. "I'm here. I'll always be here."

A sob stuck in her throat, and a fat tear fell to stain the sheet.

He let go of her hands to clasp her head and turn her to face him. "Let me in."

He lowered his head before she could make sense of the words, and his mouth grazed hers. So gentle and yet his kiss carried a bit of desperation. His tongue swept in, tasting her, making her pussy clench, then retreating. He growled and delved deeper, stronger. His cock plunged harder, higher, hitting her G-spot.

Sweet, hot, tingling pleasure burst from her center outward, but unlike the other orgasms Will had given her, this one didn't rush through her like a raging river. This one oozed through her system like a slow moving bed of lava. And instead of falling into the dark abyss, with each thrust, she rose higher, floating into the bright heavens.

From the distant heights, she heard Will's groan, felt his lips leave hers. A low, noise rumbled above her. The rocking stopped, but the rapture continued to pulse, slower, lighter, yet just as powerful.

His weight lessened, and she whimpered as he slipped away. Then he gathered her against him so that she lay half on top of him, head on his shoulder, arm across his chest, one leg over his. His heart thundered under her like a herd of wild horses, and his breath blew strands of hair in her face, but she was too content to care.

He lifted the hand over his chest and kissed her palm, then set it over his heart and covered it with his own. The fingers of his other hand trailed up and down her arm, soothing.

Their breathing slowed, and as she drifted into the much needed sleep, Texas finally understood and accepted one thing. She was falling in love with

Will.

All over again.

****

A grayish light filtered through the thin yellow curtains. The clock on the nightstand shrieked for the fifth time. Texas slapped at it until she found the off button. She sat up slowly, swung her legs over the side of the bed, and stared at the floor. Muscles rebelled and sleep fogged her brain. Two nights of little to no sleep because she'd been worried and three rounds of deliciously satisfying sex should have been enough excuse to stay in bed.

That and the extremely masculine and intensely sexy cowboy lying behind her.

But work called and there was a lot of it. And with the light of day, she had to examine the feelings she'd finally admitted to. Loving Will was a mistake, and she should have known it would happen, should have known better. Will was easy to love but hard to get over. Which only made it more important to put a stop to this thing between them.

She'd tried when he woke her the first time, but his kisses had been intoxicating, the pounding of his cock as he knelt behind her exquisite. Need overpowered logic, and she'd decided to accept the gift of one last night with Will. The third time, she'd taken the initiative, waking him with a blowjob. Of course, he hadn't let her finish, which was fine with her when he pinned her to the mattress and made love to her again, long and sweet.

Rising, she gazed down at him. She should wake him. They needed to talk. But she was already late and he looked so peaceful on his stomach, one arm behind him, the other hanging off the bed. His legs stretched diagonally across the mattress too short for his tall frame. With each moment that passed, the sun turned more yellow than gray and called attention to the gold streaks woven into the brown hair falling over his forehead.

His face was relaxed, dark lashes kissing high cheekbones. The crinkles at the corners of his eyes weren't as pronounced, and his jaw, shadowed with stubble, was slack, his bottom lip slightly parted from the top. The rest of him, though...

Even in sleep, his body looked hard, chiseled, brown from working in the sun, with a hint of underlying red from their day at the lake. The sheet covered him from the waist down, and Texas was tempted to jerk it off. But that would only add to her tardiness and to the heartache that would surely come later today.

Turning away, she headed to the shower. The hot spray felt good against her tired and well-used body. She soaped up quickly but slowed as she sudsed up the tender flesh between her legs. The scent of sex, of Will, hit her nostrils, and she tensed. They hadn't used a condom. Not that it mattered. She was on the pill, and Will wouldn't put her in harm's way.

Texas placed a hand on her lower abdomen and, for a moment, let herself imagine a tiny life there. Will's child. He'd be such a great dad, much like his own father had been. But fatherhood would be some other woman's gift to Will.

The unwelcome image of Krystal and the look on her face as she stood in Texas' office swam before her eyes. *Texas, please. I really need to talk to him. It's important.*

Oh, god, was that why she needed to talk to Will? Was she pregnant?

Bile churned in her stomach. Pregnancy meant irrevocable ties. Will tied to a woman like Krystal, another Missy who'd bleed him dry both emotionally and financially, was beyond thinkable. He'd never be happy. *And he'd never be completely yours.*

He'll never be yours, anyway, so why even go there?

Texas shut off the water along with all the fruitless speculation. Besides, as many times as she'd lectured Will on the importance of safe sex, he'd promised he was careful. And Will didn't have a careless bone in his body.

Yeah, like he'd been so careful last night?

****

Walking from the sunlit parking lot into the auction barn, Will stopped and let his eyes adjust to the fluorescent lighting. He'd meant to get up with Texas, maybe make love to her again in the shower, then feed her breakfast. She'd need it to recoup the energy he'd sapped from her during the night.

A smile pulled at his lips. He'd actually spent the night in her bed. A full night. The sex was amazing but sleeping beside her, watching her sleep... He wanted that every night. And if the way she'd looked at him when they made love was any indication, he'd have that and more.

He'd almost fucked up, though. The words I love you had been on the tip of his tongue. Hell, they'd been rolling around in his mouth all day. At the lake, he'd wanted so badly to let them out when she accused him of meeting another woman in Houston. He'd about bit his tongue clean off to hold them inside.

Wouldn't be long now. He could feel it.

Will crossed the foyer and scanned the large, open, semi-circular area made of concrete tiers with stadium seating. Texas stood with the new auctioneer on the raised dais, separated from the seating area by the small arena used to show cattle during the auction. Jeans hugged her hips and legs with a closeness he envied. Her shirt fit the curves of her waist and pulled just a bit across her breasts. The neckline rode a little lower than he was used to seeing on her, but he liked it. Maybe later he'd have a chance to take advantage of it.

She bent to show the guy—what was his name? Joey?—something on the low table and glanced up to point in his direction. He waved to catch her eye. She straightened and waved back, but her smile seemed tight. She was nervous. He'd expected that, though. She probably hadn't figured out she loved him yet.

Texas exited the dais through a side door, probably headed for her sanctuary. He made his way along the area behind the seating to join her. Her gaze darted all around him until they met at the door to her office.

"Mornin'," she said, finally meeting his eyes.

Removing his Stetson, he tried to disarm her with a smile. "Mornin'." He opened the door for her. "Hope you don't mind. I took a shower at your place rather than going all the way home."

"No, it's fine." The squeak in her voice and the pink flush on those ivory cheeks told him she was remembering why he'd had to use her shower.

He couldn't help it. He had to touch her. He reached to brush the hair from her face, but she ducked beneath his arm and into her office.

"So you're hangin' out here today?" She skirted her desk, sat down, and shuffled a few papers around.

"Don't I always?"

"Yeah. I just figured you'd have a lot to catch up on after being gone for two days and then spending yesterday at the lake and..."

And last night in your bed?

He could have teased her, but that would only make her more nervous. Instead, he plunked down in one of the chairs in front of her desk and laid his hat on the seat next to him.

"I forgot to tell you," she peered down her nose at the computer screen and palmed the mouse, "Krystal came by looking for you while you were in Houston."

The smile slipped from his face. The thought of Krystal anywhere near Texas didn't sit well. "Yeah?"

"Said she needed to talk to you. That it was important."

He grunted, his mood suddenly souring. Krystal was just like his mother. Why he hadn't seen it before was beyond him. She probably wanted money for a new whatever. "Krystal thinks a broken nail is important."

Texas finally faced him. "Is there any chance she might be pregnant?"

What the fuck? Where had that come from? Did she really think he'd be that stupid? "There's every chance she could be. But if she is, it isn't mine."

She chewed her lip for a minute. "Are you sure?"

"We've had this conversation before. I've never had sex without a condom, pill or no pill."

"You did last night."

The memory of his dick sinking into her hot, wet pussy, feeling the velvety soft tissue surround him sent blood surging to his cock and stirred thoughts of bending her over the desk and doing it again. But her accusation hit him in the gut. "I promised you a long time ago when you were preaching safe sex, I'd never take that risk. This is the second time in as many days you've let me know how little faith you have in me."

Her eyes rounded, and she sat forward, her hands sliding across the desk toward him. "I didn't mean it that way."

He lifted a brow. "How did you mean it?"

Withdrawing the gesture, she clasped her hands together and stared at them. "It's just...you didn't—I mean, *we* didn't..."

"Is that what you're worried about? That you might be pregnant?" Warmth flooded his chest. The idea of Texas carrying his son or daughter... "Would it be so bad?"

Her head snapped up, and her jaw dropped. For a minute, she didn't speak, but her expression waffled between shock, embarrassment, and confusion. What they all meant, he wasn't sure. "I don't—"

The door to her office opened, and Joey popped his head around it. "Callaghan's having a conniption fit. Wants to talk to you."

Texas stood up so fast her chair rolled into the wall with a bang. "Tell him I'll be right there."

Will caught her hand as she passed. "T?"

She hesitated then glanced down at him with that deer in the headlights look.

He let his thumb circle her palm. "We'll talk later tonight."

With a nod, she tugged free and walked out the door.

The morning sure hadn't gone as he'd planned. Nothing he couldn't iron out, though.

A smile played on his lips. He couldn't help wishing Texas wasn't on the pill. Watching her belly grow with their baby inside her would make every dream he'd ever had come true. And she'd have to marry him then.

Will chuckled. Nothing like putting the horse before the cart.

Chapter Eight

Texas fumbled with the keys as she locked up the barn for the night and headed for the bar. She was a jumpy as a long-tailed cat in a roomful of rocking chairs. She really didn't want to meet Will, but she didn't want to be alone with him, either. She wouldn't be able to control herself.

Every time she'd turned around today, he'd been right there, standing too close, laying a hand on her waist or shoulder, touching her hand or face as they talked to neighbors and friends or while she tried to work. Her nerves were frayed. Her body was hungry. Hell, she was so turned on, not just her panties were wet. Her jeans were, too.

And damn it, he was confusing her. A baby? What was he thinking? From the expression on his face, he'd actually liked the idea. It reminded her of the way he'd looked at her the night before as they made love.

Sex. They'd had sex. Will wasn't the kind of man to make love. Was he? She'd never thought about it one way or the other, tried not to. Will might have dated a lot of women, but with the exception of Krystal and one or two others, he'd steered clear of long-term relationships. It stood to reason those few meant something to him. At the very least, more than she did. After all, she was merely a friendly convenience, a...a fuck buddy.

The term made her cringe and nearly turned her around. So crude, so ugly, so emotionless. Only the thought of returning their status to *just friends* kept her feet moving. Falling deeper in love with him wasn't an option.

Shouldering through the door, Texas spotted Will at the bar, all long and lean and sexy as hell. She swallowed the rising panic and made her way through the maze of tables and past the dance floor. He caught her reflection in the mirror and swiveled on the stool to face her with a grin she was sure melted every panty in the bar.

Her heart skipped a beat, despite her resolve to keep him at a distance. Damn it.

He stood and bent to kiss her forehead. He had to stop doing that. "What took you so long?"

Shrugging, she slid onto the stool he'd saved for her. "Stuff."

"I told you I'd wait." He sat down beside her. "I don't like you walking in the dark by yourself."

"I've done it a million times." So why the concern now? No, she wouldn't let herself read anything into it.

Will motioned to the bartender and pointed to Texas. A beer appeared on the bar in front of her. She slugged back a couple of gulps then set it down and picked up a napkin to keep her hands busy. No way was she getting drunk tonight.

After she'd shredded one, she started on another. "Look, Will, we need to talk."

He lowered his beer and spun on the stool, his knee brushing her thigh and stopping at her hip. "Yes, we do. But we're not talking here."

Texas peeked under her lashes. He sounded as serious as she felt. Maybe she'd read him wrong and the talk about babies had woken him up. Good. That would make this conversation easier.

She nodded, released a deep breath, and allowed herself to take another drink. For the first time since she'd walked in the door, she heard the music and realized how crowded the place was. The dance floor was full. A live band was in the house.

Will rested an elbow on the bar and his beer on his thigh, still too close for comfort. He scanned the crowd. "So how'd it go, today?"

The question did what it was meant to—start the comfortable and safe chitchat. She could do that. "We had a good one. Other than Callaghan and his ego."

"He's always been an ass."

"True." Texas smiled and lifted the longneck to her lips. A body slammed into her from behind and the bottle clinked hard against her teeth. Beer spilled down her shirt. "Shit, who—"

"I've been looking all over for you." The voice was easily recognized. She'd heard it in her office four days ago.

Texas ignored the bartender's attempt to hand her a towel as Krystal wedged her skinny hips between Will's legs, her back to Texas. Krystal's hands slid along the top of Will's thighs. Texas' stomach sank even as her temper flared. Yet she had no right to be angry. He didn't belong to her. And after all, she was about to end what little there was between them.

"I've been right here." He picked up Krystal's hands and placed them on her hips, and Texas uncurled her fingers from around the longneck before she broke the bottle over the bitch's empty head. "What do you want?"

"Don't be like that, baby." There went those wandering hands again, this time skimming up his chest and around his neck. "I want to talk."

Texas believed Will when he said he'd been careful, but whatever Krystal had to say, Texas couldn't sit here and watch the woman climb all over him. As much as it pained her to think of them together or how much she wanted to scratch out those damn doe eyes, maybe it would best if Will's focus was drawn back to someone else. Not better for him if Krystal was that someone, but better for Texas.

"You can have my seat." She spun the other direction and stood. Before she could step from between the stools, Will stretched out his leg to block her with his booted foot. She shot a glare in his direction, but he was already moving. Taking hold of Krystal's wrists, he lowered his leg and swung the woman from between his thighs into the aisle.

Rising, he gave Texas a pointed look that froze her on the spot. He turned his attention to Krystal. "Are you pregnant?"

"What? No. Who told you that?" Krystal narrowed her eyes on Texas.

Will lifted a brow at Texas that said "see?" and didn't bother looking back at the woman as he asked, "Got some disease I should know about?"

Krystal gasped. "No, of course not. I don't know where you're getting—"

"Then we have nothing to talk about." He let go of her, stepped toward Texas, and grabbed her hand. "Dance with me."

"I don't think that's a good idea." Texas tried to get loose, but he pulled her against him. Her breasts clashed with his chest, and like chocolate in the hot summer sun, her insides turned to goo.

"She can't follow me on the dance floor." His irritation with Krystal was evident, but the fierce frown he gave Texas hurt, as did his explanation. He wanted her to be his cover. Wasn't the first time, but if she had anything to do with it, it would be the last.

"Okay." She let him lead her onto the dance floor and into his arms. Big mistake. If she'd have been paying attention, she would have stalled him and waited for a faster song.

He twirled her around then drew her in close, leaving not a breath of air between them. He began a slow and sexy two-step. One hand smoothed up her back, the other flattened just above her ass. Neither offered room for resistance. Not that her damn body would allow it. Her nipples practically stabbed his chest, and her pussy was wet and grinding on the thigh between her legs. Traitor.

The floor was crowded, and she recognized a few couples. Harper and Josh danced closer.

Will chose that moment to feather his lips along

her jaw, tracing a path toward her lips. Her first instinct was to meet him half way, but Texas turned her head aside. "Don't."

He eased back enough to frown at her again but didn't say a word.

Harper smiled and Josh gave them a goofy grin and a thumbs up.

Well, hell, Will would have everyone in the bar thinking they were a couple.

"I'm sorry." And she really was. Sorry she had to stop him. Sorry she'd let things get this far. Sorry they couldn't go further. Sorry she loved him. "I appreciate the fact you're trying to show Krystal it's over, but people are getting the impression there's something going on between us."

"And they'd be right." His expression dared her to say otherwise.

Well, yes, but she'd meant something romantic. The familiar sting behind her eyes signaled a meltdown on the horizon. She slid her hands from around Will's neck to his chest and gave him a gentle yet determined nudge. "I can't do this here."

He stepped back, releasing all but her hand. "Fine. Let's go to your house."

She shook her head. They'd go home, he'd kiss her, and she'd be lost.

"Then come home with me tonight."

Tonight. He said it as if her staying was a forgone conclusion. And he was right. When it came to saying no to Will, her willpower was non-existent. She needed to find some neutral ground. Maybe this *was* the best place to tell him. She had to get her shit together first. "I have to use the restroom."

"I'll wait at the bar." He let go of her hand, and she made her escape.

Several of the guys from the auction barn nodded and said hello as she skirted the pool tables to get to the bathrooms. Jarod leaned on a stick but straightened when he saw her. He tipped his hat in a hello, but his expression was anything but friendly.

Damn, that was all she needed, another confrontation. She had yet to get through the one with Will.

Ignoring Jarod, she ducked into the ladies' room and sank against the wall. Rubbing her hands over her face, she drove her fingers through her hair, clutched a handful, and resisted the urge to scream.

Across the small space, her reflection stared back at her. Arms dropping to her sides, she stepped closer and leaned against the sink for a closer inspection. Her cheeks were flushed, and red rimmed her eyes. She looked like shit.

"Well, Texas, you've got yourself in one big fucking mess." And how long could she hide from it. Not long enough. Even if she did camp out in the restroom, sooner or later Will would simply come in looking for her.

Hell, why should she be so worried? He might be a little too caught up in this friends-with-fringe-benefits relationship, with all the PDA, but it was mostly about the convenience for him. He'd probably take her decision to put things back to rights with a shrug and start the search for a new conquest. She should just get it over with and get the hell home.

Gathering her anger for strength, she turned on the water and splashed cold water on her face, hoping to relieve some of the blotchy redness on her otherwise white face. She grabbed for a paper towel, but of course, the machine was empty. The front of her shirt would have to do, beer stains and all.

After smoothing the mess she'd made of her hair, Texas opened the bathroom door.

Harper waited on the other side. "Are you okay?"

"Yeah, just a little tired."

"If you want to talk…" Harper offered.

Texas just wanted to go home. She forced a smile. "Maybe lunch this week."

"Sounds great." Harper pointed to the bathroom door. "My turn."

Texas sidestepped to let Harper past, then sucked in a deep breath and let it out slowly. She turned and plowed right into a brick wall.

No, not a wall. Jarod. Had he been waiting for her?

He dug his fingers into her arms and backed her against the wall to the right of the door. A mixture of bourbon and beer assailed her nostrils. Jarod wasn't a drinker. "Jarod?"

He leaned closer. "I saw you, you know. You and Will in the parking lot the night of the town meeting."

"What?" He'd seen them? If she thought her face was red before, nothing compared to the fiery heat of mortification blazing there now. How much had he seen? Did it matter?

"Thought you were upset so I followed you outside." He barked a bitter laugh. "Guess the joke's on me, huh?"

The hurt in his voice triggered the guilt she'd felt at breaking up with him. It was worse now that she knew how much it hurt to love someone who'd never love her in return. "I'm sorry."

"Me, too." His eyes softened and fingers loosened around her arms as he wobbled back a step. But with his next alcohol-laced breath, his face hardened again. "How long has this been going on, anyway? Were you fucking him behind my back?"

"Jarod, don't do this." She reached to steady him. "Let me get you home."

He slapped her hand away, then grabbed her again. "You think I want you now. After what I saw? The two of you fucking like animals?"

Texas didn't blame him for his anger, but she sure as hell didn't have to put up with his drunken abuse. Besides, people were beginning to take notice.

She shoved at him, but his grip wouldn't give. "Let go of me."

"I should have known. That's the reason you dumped me, isn't it." He shook her. "Because of Will. It's always been Will. You compared me to him at every turn. You're in love with him, aren't you?"

The fact he'd guessed at her feelings for Will took her off guard, and the truth hit her smack in the face. She had compared him to Will. She'd compared every man to Will. She hadn't fallen in love with him. She'd never stopped.

"See. You can't even deny it."

"What's going on?" Will's deep voice behind her resonated with anger, but all she could think about was whether he'd overheard Jarod's accusation.

Jarod must have heard the threat in Will's voice because he released her.

She turned to Will. "Nothing. Let's go."

Will's fury-glazed eyes remained on Jarod. She'd never seen him this mad. It was a little scary.

She laid a hand on his chest. "Will."

He looked down at her and nodded. With a hand at her back, he turned them to go.

"Yeah, go on," Jarod bellowed in a drunken slur. "She's yours now. I wouldn't touch the slut."

The hand at her back fell away, and before she could turn around, the sound of flesh hitting flesh drowned out the music, the crash of a break on the pool table, and the ping-ping-ping of starships guns killing aliens on the nearby video machines. Jarod was on the floor, blood trickling from his mouth, and Will stood over him.

Texas blinked at Jarod, then at Will. "What the hell did you do that for?"

Will flexed the fingers of his right hand, then cradled it in the other. "He's lucky I don't do more."

Elbowing him away, she squatted next to Jarod. "Somebody get me a towel and some ice."

God help her, she wanted to knock both their heads together. But she couldn't blame either of them. This was her fault. She'd done this. Driven a good man to drink and a gentle man to violence. And if things didn't change soon, she'd drive herself insane.

Or maybe she was already there.

****

Will clenched his jaw, fighting the blinding rage inside him. His hand hurt like hell. He might have broken a bone on Jarod's face. And there was Texas, kneeling beside the fucker, holding a rag to his face, and glaring at Will as if this was all his fault.

"You didn't have to hit him. He's drunk." She turned her back to him and lifted the rag to gauge the damage.

"You broke my tooth," Jarod shouted and tried to stand up.

"Careful, now." Her tone grew soft, soothing as she put her arm around Jarod to help him rise.

"Get off me." Jarod flung his arm out, knocking her against the chairs behind them, and Will saw red again.

In two steps, he was on Jarod, grabbing him by the collar and hauling him off the floor. Drunk or not, the son of a bitch deserved a beating.

"Will, stop." Texas tugged on his arm, but he shrugged her loose. "To hell with both of assholes."

He wanted to pound the shit out of Jarod, but that wouldn't win any points with Texas. Instead, he shoved the bastard against the same wall he'd backed her into earlier. "If you ever touch her again, I swear I'll break more than just a tooth."

"Let go," Josh pried his hands from Jarod's shirt, and Jarod slid to the floor. "Come on, man. Harper'll be out any minute, and she'd going to haul your ass to jail." Then he pointed to a couple of guys. "Get

Jarod home so he can sleep it off."

Will stepped over the man's legs and scanned the growing crowd for Texas. She was gone. Somebody handed him his hat as he caught sight of her striding out the door. He didn't stick around to for a chat with the sheriff. Harper knew where to find him.

Adrenaline pumped through him, driving him out the door. She was half way down the trail to the barn, and even from here he could tell she was pissed by her angry stride. His boots kicked up gravel as he sprinted after her.

Closing the distance between them at the edge of the barn's parking lot, Will yelled, "Texas, wait."

She only quickened her steps. "Go away, Will."

He reached her side just under the light pole near the barn. "What are you mad at me for?"

"Seriously?" She threw up her arms and let them flop to her sides. "You get into a barroom brawl, and you want to know why I'm mad?"

"I won't have him talking to you like that." A sudden thought seized him. He grabbed her arm and spun her around, ignoring the pain in his hand. "Are you in love with him?"

"What? No, I told you I wasn't."

She shrugged to get loose, but he tightened his grip. "Then why are you defending him?"

"He saw us, Will. In the parking lot. In your truck." Her voice rose with every word, anger, guilt, and humiliation all fighting for control.

Damn Jarod to hell. Will wished the son of a bitch was here so he could hit him again for making

Texas feel this way. "How much did he see?"

"Enough to know what was going on." She took a deep breath and let it out. And with it, her anger seemed to dissipate. Moisture welled in her eyes. She opened her mouth, but nothing came out. She swallowed, then whispered, "He's hurting, Will. I hurt him."

Shit. If he could start the night over and change the way he'd handled things, he would, no matter how much satisfaction he'd gained from punching Jarod. He hated the guilt she felt for hurting the son of a bitch, yet that was part of what made her the woman she was. The woman he loved. He drew her against him. "You couldn't have known he'd see us."

"Don't you get it?" She flattened her hands on his chest and leaned away. "We've been careless, behaving like a couple of teenagers. And he was right. I've been acting like a slut."

"Don't you dare talk about yourself like that." He shook her gently. "And don't let him or anyone else cheapen what we have."

A tear rolled down her cheek, followed quickly by another. "What *do* we have, Will? A few hot and sweaty moments? A fast, hard fuck when the mood strikes?"

Will's head jerked back, the sting of her words like a slap in the face. His lungs seized, refusing to draw his next breath. "Is that all it was to you?"

Even as he asked the question, he knew it wasn't. She felt something for him. He was sure of it.

Her eyes rounded and filled with remorse. She

looked as stricken as he felt. "No. I'm sorry. I didn't mean that." Her fingers curled into his shirt. "But don't you see? We can't keep doing this. We're ruining everything. Just look at us."

"Nothing is ruined. It's better. The past week has been the best in my life. I—" He swallowed hard, knowing now was probably the worst time to tell her but… "I love you, Texas."

Setting those three little words free after more than a decade of choking on them felt good. They felt right. The expression on her face…not so much. Surprise, he'd expected and prepared for when imaging this moment. After the shock, he'd thought her green eyes might brighten as she confessed she loved him, too. Other times, though, especially after Jarod had shown him the damn engagement ring, Will had pictured pity clouding her eyes as she told him she could never love him.

But the pain contorting her face now, and the panic… Fuck.

"No." She shook her head. "You might think you're in love with me, Will, but you're not. In lust maybe, but not love." She stepped back, shook her head again, and bolted for her house.

That was it? He'd told her he loved her, and she was dismissing him? As if he threw those words around every fucking day?

"I think I know my own goddam mind," he called after her, then followed, his anger growing with every stride up the walk. "And let me tell you something, Texas Tallulah Taylor. You couldn't be more wrong."

"What if I'm right?" Keys in hand, she made quick work of the lock.

"You're not."

"But what if I am?" She opened the door and turned to block his entry. "I know you care about me. But it's not the same. And even if it were, what happens to me when the new wears off and you get bored and move on to newer, greener pastures?"

Hadn't she heard a word he'd said? He was beginning to think she didn't know him at all.

"Goodnight, Will." She started to shut the door, but instinct—or maybe it was desperation—took over, and he stuck his boot between the door and the jamb before it closed.

"I'm not done." With the quickness that made her squeal and jump out of the way, he flung the door wide. It hit the wall with a bang. Letting his gut lead him, he hauled her against his chest and whirled to pin her against the still rattling glass insert. "I won't let you shut me out."

Her lips parted, and her gaze dropped to his mouth as he lowered his head and tasted her like he'd wanted to do all night. She whimpered, and her tongue welcomed his, drawing him in. The tang of the beer she'd been drinking blended with her own unique flavor. Her arms circled his neck to pull him in tighter, one hand diving under his hat and knocking it to the floor.

Will leaned his weight into her, savoring her softness. Her full firm breasts mashed into his chest, tempting him, and though he knew he had to maintain control, he couldn't resist touching them.

He slid a hand from her waist and up her ribs to knead the supple mound. It filled his palm and then some.

She moaned and arched into him, her hips tilting, her pussy riding the thigh he'd shoved between her legs. The motion wasn't lost on his dick, either, already hard and straining against his zipper.

He groaned and shifted his hand back to her waist. As much as he wanted to fuck her against the damn door until she screamed his name, he needed her to listen, to hear and believe him when he said he loved her. And he needed her to admit she loved him, too. Because she did, goddamnit.

He slowed the heated frenzy of the kiss. His tongue retreated, then his lips, but only enough that his mouth hovered a breath away from hers. "I know how I feel, and it's not just lust." Her body tensed beneath his, and he lifted his head for a better look at her reaction. She searched his face, and he could see the battle waging inside her. "I love you, and I promise I'm not going anywhere."

"It's what you do, Will." The resignation in her voice sounded too much like defeat and not the surrender he'd hoped for. "You've never had a girlfriend longer than six months, and that's a stretch. Krystal is the perfect example."

So, there it was. It wasn't the fact that she didn't love him. She just didn't trust him. She'd said as much by the lake when she accused him of meeting another woman in Houston. And again today with the possibility of him getting Krystal pregnant.

And why should she trust him? Every time he'd

taken another woman to bed, he'd given her another reason not to. *Greener pastures.* That's what she thought they were. Well, maybe it was time for her to know the truth. The whole truth.

Will nodded, more as confirmation of his thoughts than her accusation. "So, I'm just some horny bull eager to put his seed in every cow in the barn?"

She frowned up at him. "No, that's not—"

"I get it." He eased back, tugged her away from the door, and slammed it shut, letting a little of his anger and hurt show. "You know me so well."

"Will?" Her eyes rounded, and she backed up two steps to his one. Good. At least she knew he meant business.

"Well, little miss know it all." He continued to herd her into the living room though he'd rather herd her up the stairs and into bed. Then he'd show her horny bull. "You want to know why I broke up with Krystal?"

She tipped her chin toward the ceiling. "You said she was cheating, sexting other men."

"Yeah, well, I lied." Sarcasm rolled off his tongue as he lifted a shoulder and let it drop.

"You've been doing that a lot lately." Her ass met the sofa. She darted a glance from the left to the right then back at him. "How am I supposed to believe anything you say?"

"Well, here's the biggest lie of all. One I've been living for a long time." He stopped as his boot tips bumped hers. He braced both hands on the couch and invaded her space. "I didn't just magically fall in love with you because we had sex. I've been in love with you since the day we kissed behind your god damn house."

"You're right. That is a lie." She snorted. "You looked at me like I was some stranger you'd never seen before."

The memory of that day came back in a rush of sweet torture. Her face, fresh and dappled with spots of sunlight coming through the leaves of the mimosa tree overhead. The way her smile had turned shy as their eyes met and he ducked his head to kiss her. The sweetness of her lips...

"You were." His anger faded as he palmed her face and brushed a thumb over those same lips. He smiled at the tremor his touch caused. "Before I kissed you, you were my best friend, the girl I'd known for most of my life. Then suddenly, you were someone else. Someone I didn't recognize. Mysterious, sexy, the most beautiful girl in the world. It scared the hell out of me and, at the same time, felt like the most exciting and natural thing. Then you shrugged me off like a failed science experiment."

She lowered her gaze to his chest, making it impossible to read her feelings. "That was a long time ago."

"Yes, it was. And all that time, I tried to tell myself I could get over you, that I could stop loving you. That's the reason for all the women. I thought for sure I'd fall in love with one of them." He lowered his hands to his side and backed away a few feet. Touching her was too distracting. It made him want more and that was what started this whole thing.

He leaned against the arch between the foyer and living room. "I didn't start this thing between us because I wanted to have sex with you."

A smile pulled at his lips at the lie and at the pink staining her cheeks as she crossed her arms over her chest as if she could hide her arousal so easily.

"Well, I did, but..." He shrugged again, unwilling to apologize. "After you dumped Jarod, I thought maybe the time was right, that I hadn't missed my chance. I had this big plan to make you fall in love with me that didn't involve sexting or back seats. But then you told me about that guy sexting you, and well...I saw an opening and I took it.

"I thought sexting and hot sex was what you wanted. I wanted to show you the passion we could share, but more than that, I hoped you'd look past our friendship and finally see how much I love you. How happy we could be. I want a life with you, T. Kids, grandkids, the whole shebang. I've never wanted that with anyone else."

Will straightened and crossed the distance between them, trying to hide the desperation rising inside him. She still seemed so confused, and he wasn't sure he was getting through. "I love you. *Only* you. I've never said those words to any woman." Not even his mother after he realized she'd never return the affection and wouldn't want his love even if he offered it. She only wanted money.

"Hell, I even sold Crusher for you—for us. What more can I say or do to make you believe me?"

Fresh tears welled in her eyes. She licked her lips but still wouldn't look at him. "I want to, but..."

He ground his teeth as the pain of her rejection sliced through him. "But you can't?"

"I don't know." She laid a hand on his chest. "I need time to think, to figure things out."

The tightness under her hand was suffocating. His body felt like lead, but he forced a nod. "That's fine." What else could he say or do? He'd spilled his guts, confessed everything, and still she didn't trust him. He nodded again, just to convince himself time would change that, though, at the moment, he didn't hold out much hope. "When you figure it out, you know where to find me."

He turned and walked to the front entry to retrieve his hat. Opening the door, he stopped and stared out at the darkness that looked an awful lot like his future. Dark and void of the only woman he'd ever wanted. That's what it would be, too, because now that he'd had a taste of what it would be like with her as more than a friend, he sure as hell couldn't go back.

Swallowing the bitter lump lodged in his throat, he shifted to one side in the doorway and stared at a rusty hinge. It blurred for a moment, he blinked, and it cleared. "Don't take too long, T. I won't wait another fifteen years. I can't. Not after what we've shared."

He dusted the brim of his hat and placed it on his head. One hand on the knob, he had to clarify one thing. "I didn't break up with Krystal because she was cheating. That was just an excuse, not the reason."

From the corner of his eye, he saw Texas step closer. "Tell me."

Will finally looked at her, letting all the love in his heart show. "She wasn't you."

Chapter Nine

Texas woke to a pounding in her head. She curled into a ball and buried her face in the pillow she'd hugged all night. The citrusy scent of Will's cologne filled her senses, and another round of tears leaked from sore and swollen lids. Memories of her argument with him splashed across them in living color.

She squeezed her eyes tighter to make the images go away. It hurt too much, and she just wanted to slip back into the dark relief of sleep. Instead, the heavy weight of loss threatened to suffocate her as it had the entire night. Every time she'd thought she couldn't take another breath, she reached for the phone only to realize she had no one to call.

Will was her best friend, and she'd lost him.

The pounding started again, but this time it wasn't in her head. It came from downstairs.

Texas bolted upright. *Will.*

She threw off the sheet and sprang out of bed, half tripping on the sheets tangled around her ankle. Not bothering to put a robe over her nightshirt, she dashed down the stairs. *Will.*

Halfway to the door, her heart dropped to her stomach and her feet slowed. The outline through the beveled glass in the door was too narrow and not as tall, the shade of hair too light. *Jarod.*

Or course it wasn't Will. Why would it be? He'd shared his feelings, told her he loved her and wanted a life with her. And she believed *he* believed that, but she hadn't been able to—still couldn't—translate any of what he'd said into a future. All she saw was heartache and the end of their friendship. And she'd pretty much guaranteed both.

Jarod put his hand above his eyes and his face to the glass. He straightened when he saw her. There was no pretending she wasn't home.

Opening the door, she half hid behind it. "Jarod."

The skin around his jaw was a dark bluish-purple, and one side of his busted lip was swollen twice its normal size. The other side lifted in a tentative smile that wavered. "Can I come in?"

The last thing she wanted to do was deal with Jarod, but she felt too sorry for him to say no. She opened the door wider. "Sure."

He waited for her to close it then followed her into the living room and sat on the edge of the sofa.

"Can I get you something to drink?" She could use a cup of coffee.

"No, thanks. I won't be long." His Adam's apple warbled in his throat as she sat on the chair kitty-corner from him. "I came to apologize for last night. I wasn't myself."

"You have nothing to be sorry for." He might have been an ass, but she understood his pain. More than she cared to. She reached for his hand. "I'm the one who's sorry."

"No, I had no right to say those things." He tried another smile and winced. "At least we know what kind of drunk I'd be."

"Yeah, you shouldn't go there again." She gave his hand a light squeeze then released it, sat back, and indicated his nose with the jerk of her chin. "Does it hurt?

"Like hell. But it's very much deserved." His gaze roved over her face. "Minus bruises, you don't look much better. You okay?"

Her hands automatically flew to her hair, smoothing it from her face. "I just woke up?"

He glanced at his watch but didn't say anything.

Texas checked the clock on the mantel. Eleven fifty-two. She wasn't a late sleeper, always up with the sun, something he'd know. "I didn't get much sleep last night." At his pained expression, she realized how he might interpret that, in light of what he'd seen the night of the town meeting. "It's not what you think. Will and I had a fight."

"So you're together now?"

"I—no. I wouldn't say that." She blinked as the prickling in her nose forewarned more tears. Will had always been her best friend, but after what they'd done this week, after last night… "I really don't know what we are, but—" God, what was she thinking? Jarod was the last person she could or should talk to about Will. "I just want you to know I wasn't with him while we were together. I wasn't cheating on you. I promise this only started a week ago. And we're…"

Over.

"That's where you're wrong. It's been going on for years." Jarod lifted a hand before she could argue. "Maybe not the sex, but there's always been something between you, a connection I could never understand. I didn't realize how deep it went. I thought if I loved you enough, you'd eventually…"

"I'm sorry. I never meant to hurt you." If he felt half as shitty as she did, the apology wasn't worth a damn.

"No, I should have known when I showed Will the ring and told him I was going to propose. His reaction said it all. Yeah, he was positive, encouraging even, telling me to make you happy or he'd kick my ass and turning white as a ghost with every word. Guess that's why it took me a month to build up the nerve. I knew in my gut you were going to say no."

All that time, Will knew Jarod was going to propose? He'd never said a word or given her any warning. No, that's when he'd pulled away, grown quiet and distant, and she'd blamed it on his breakup with Krystal.

"He loves you, Texas. But I guess you know that. I hope things work out for you. And Will. He's a good guy. He'll make you happy."

He already had. He always had. He'd been there for her through every crisis—her mom, her dad, having to take over the business. He'd been her rock. Yet, never in a million years would she have imagined his feelings for her were more than friendship. His admission had taken her by complete surprise.

I've been in love with you since the day we kissed behind your fucking house.

Everything he'd said last night was from the heart. And she'd known, felt it as sure as her own heart ached to believe him, yearned to say yes, that she loved him, too. But the enormity of his confession had been too much to take in. Her emotions had been all over the place, and she'd clung to the doubt and fear like a safety line.

All she could see now was Will and how he'd stood in the door, hat in hand, his beautiful eyes so lost and brimming with unshed tears. She hadn't seen him cry but once, the day he'd buried his dad. If she'd hurt him that much…

God, why hadn't she stopped him from leaving?

Because she was too afraid of destroying their friendship, afraid of getting hurt. But her fear went deeper than that. Everyone she'd ever loved had left her. By admitting she loved Will and accepting that he loved her, she risked losing him. But she'd been a fool and ended up doing that anyway.

"I've lost him." She hugged her waist and doubled over as a sob shook her.

"Awe, hell." Jarod scooped her up and settled her on his lap on the sofa. "It's okay. Let it all out." He mopped at her face with a handkerchief. "Everything will be okay."

"Y-you didn't see the look on his fa-ace." She couldn't quell the raging sense of loss overwhelming her. Nor could she stop the words from tumbling out. "I practically called him a l-liar. I accused him of being a horny bull." She grabbed a handful of his shirt. "He said he sold Crusher...for *me*." Which made no sense at all. "Why would he do that?"

He handed her the handkerchief. "I thought he did it for his mother."

Well, that made even less sense. "I don't know, but I should have a-asked." She blew her nose and laid her head on his shoulder. "I should have told him I loved him."

Jarod rubbed her back in slow soothing circles. "You still can."

"What if it's too late?"

"What? He's going to fall out of love with you overnight?" He snorted, then groaned and reached for his jaw. "Believe me, it's not that easy."

With a hiccup, she angled her head to stare up at him. He was a good man. Just not a very good drunk. "I'm so sorry." She sniffled. "You deserve someone so much better than me."

"You can't choose who you love, Texas, so don't feel guilty." He kissed the top of her head. "I just hope I find someone who loves me as much as you love Will."

"Me, too."

"Just give him a call." He tucked a tangled strand behind her ear. "Tell him how you feel and all this, the fight and whatever was said, will be forgotten in no time. You'll see."

"I hope so."

"I should go so you can get yourself cleaned up. You don't want him seeing you in this ratty old T-shirt, all red-faced and snotty, do you?"

Texas laughed then sniffed again. "No."

But looking down at her old nightshirt, she realized Will wouldn't have called it ratty. In fact, he seemed to like it. Just like he liked her white cotton panties.

Because he loves you.

Warmth spread through Texas, dissolving the fear and doubt, replacing them with happiness and a desperate need to see Will. To tell him she'd been stupid, that she believed him, that she wanted all the things he'd mentioned — the whole shebang. It wasn't too late. He'd forgive her for being so stupid. And maybe they'd have makeup sex.

Thoughts of Will and sex made her uncomfortably aware of her position. She had a past with Jarod, had shared a bed with him, so she was pretty sure Will wouldn't like her sitting on his lap practically naked.

As if jolted by a cattle prod, she climbed off his lap and stood. Jarod jumped up as well, obviously feeling the same awkwardness of the moment. He rounded the couch. "I'll let myself out."

"Wait," she said, something he'd said niggling in the back of her brain. "Why did you think he sold Crusher for his mother?"

A grimace tugged at one corner of his mouth and wrinkled his brow. "I probably shouldn't have said that."

"But you know something."

For a minute, she didn't think he would tell her, but then he sighed. "All I'll say is that a cashier's check made payable to Melissa Sanderson crossed my desk and it was no small chunk of change. Definitely more than he got for his bull."

Fifty head of cattle more? Shit, Missy must have been in some kind of trouble to warrant that kind of cash. Why else would Will sell his prize bull? *Hell, I even sold Crusher for you—for us.* But how would giving that bitch money benefit them? *I give her money to get rid of her. It works. I don't think I'll see her again.*

Holy shit. He didn't just give her money. He'd paid her off. For good. For them. But why? Just one of the many things they had to talk about.

She met Jarod at the door and stood on tiptoe to kiss his cheek. "Thanks."

"You're welcome. But remember, you didn't hear it from me."

When the door closed behind him, Texas headed upstairs, humbled by the day's revelations but still trying to put all the pieces together. Will knowing about Jarod's proposal. Buying off Missy. And his confessions the night before, the most important that he loved her, sacrificed so much for her. She must have been blind not to see it before. They could have been together all this time, happy, making love every night, chasing little brown-haired Wills around the house all day. They'd wasted so much time.

Not a minute more.

She went straight to her phone and dialed his number, but the call went to voicemail. She hung up without leaving a message. They had a lot to talk about, and what she had to say needed said in person.

But Jarod was right. She didn't want Will to see her in such a mess.

As she soaked in the tub, during which she shaved all the appropriate places and rested an ice pack on her face, a plan formed. If things went the way she hoped, they'd spend the rest of the night making up for lost time.

A half hour later, she stood in front of the mirror in her hot pink thong. Will might like the white cotton panty girl she was most of the time, but this situation called for the other Texas, the one he'd helped her find. The Texas who let down her hair and went a little wild. The Texas who wasn't afraid.

One last stroke of mascara, a fluff of her hair, and she picked up her phone to type a text—or rather a sext—she hoped Will would understand. With a shuddering breath, she hit send and let it fly.

****

Will walked out of the clinic and into the heat, which only added to his foul mood. That and the fact he'd fractured the middle bone of his right hand on that son of a bitch's face. It had throbbed all night, not that he'd slept anyway. He'd stared at his phone, hoping it would ring. It hadn't.

Working the fingers of his left hand into the right front pocket of his jeans, he fished for the keys to his truck. The awkward angle made it difficult since he couldn't get his hand all the way inside. Fuck, why hadn't he thought ahead and put them in his left pocket?

Giving up, he punched Texas' birthday into the

keypad outside the door and opened the truck door. Climbing inside the cab, he pulled out his phone.

He slid a finger over the screen to view notifications. His heart skipped a beat at a missed call from Texas on the top of the list. She hadn't left a message, so he had no idea whether her call was good news or bad. Or if he should call her back.

Sweat rolled down his back, forcing him to put the phone aside and get the truck started. Without thinking, he pushed the start button with his injured hand, and pain ricocheted up his arm. Another task he took for granted and struggled to accomplish. A blast of a/c hit him as the engine turned over.

Ping.

Will scrambled for the phone then hesitated. Had she made a decision? Surely, she wouldn't have called just to say otherwise. And would she really text a fuck off?

No, that wasn't Texas.

Swallowing hard, Will opened the text. The tension in his muscles lessened, his lips quirked upward, and his cock expanded to semi-erect.

T: *Still dreaming about a bj?*

Texas had never been a game player so Will took her text as a good sign, that she was using the question as a way to break the ice, just as he had sexted her a week ago to get things rolling. And just like she had, he'd play along. He sent a reply.

Will: *Always.*

The seconds that passed seemed like hours.

Finally, a new balloon popped up.

T: *Then don't make me wait 15 years to make it real.*

Will: *I'll be there in 15 mins.*

With his left hand, he threw the truck in reverse and backed up. Not that he was in a hurry to take her up on her offer. That could wait. What he wanted most was to hear her say she believed him and loved him, too.

But as he drove up to her house and parked, memories of the last few days wriggled in to mess with his confidence. What if he was wrong and she only wanted sex? She liked it a lot, responded so eagerly. No, she wouldn't do that. Not with the way they'd left things. Still, what if she thought sex was the answer to their problems? With his dick hard and imprinting itself on the teeth of his zipper, he wasn't sure he could resist whatever seduction she might have planned.

He keyed in a text.

Will: *I'm here. Meet me on the porch.*

T: *I'm not giving you a bj on the front porch.*

Will: *I'm not coming inside.* He groaned as he realized how that could be misconstrued and remembered exactly how it felt to find release inside her warm welcoming heat. Yeah, going in the house with her was a bad idea.

Another text chimed its arrival.

T: *Not even for my hot pink panties?*

Will: *I didn't come here for sex.*

T: *That's too bad. We have 15 years to make up for.*

Before he could reply, Texas stepped out the front door fully clothed—thank god—and leaned against it. She wore a peach-colored tank that would no doubt complement her ivory skin were he close enough to see. Her hair fell over her shoulders in soft waves, stealing gold from the hot afternoon sun. Her feet were bare, as were her long slender legs that stretched up to the hem of the sexy denim skirt she'd worn to the town meeting. Would he find white cotton underneath or the hot pink satin she'd promised?

Definitely a wise decision to stay outside.

Will killed the engine and slid from his truck. Halfway up the walk, his heart began to pound and his chest tightened. The sorrowful expression on her face didn't match the sexts she'd sent and more of his confidence slipped.

He stopped at the bottom of the porch steps, then slowly took them one at a time. At the top, he waited for a sign. Anything to let him know which way things would go. He didn't have to wait long.

Eyes watering, she flew toward him, launching her slender body against his. He caught her and crushed her to him as she buried her nose in the crook of his neck. As good as it felt to have her in his arms again, a yearning so strong his knees almost buckled had him backing up to lean against the closest post.

Please don't let those be tears of good-bye.

Her breath hitched, warm against his skin. "I'm sorry."

"Shh, baby," he murmured and squeezed her tighter. "It's okay."

And it would be no matter what she'd decided. He'd told her he couldn't go back to being friends, but hell if he could imagine life without Texas.

Friends with or without benefits was a damn sight better than nothing.

"I don't like it when we fight," she murmured.

"Me, either." Though he couldn't remember a time they'd ever had a serious argument.

"I was so confused. You never said a word."

His biggest mistake.

Her arms loosened and slid down his chest. She lifted her head and leaned back. Wet tracks trailing down her cheeks tore at his gut. "Why didn't you ever say something? Why wait until now?"

Will sighed and laid his hands on her waist to set her aside.

She gasped and grabbed this right arm. "Oh, god, you're hurt."

"I'm fine." Or was he? That depended on her.

"Let's go inside, in the air conditioning. You'll be more comfortable."

Um, no. He took her hand and led her to the swing at the end of the porch. It was cooler there in the shade of a white crepe myrtle. She sat beside him, her hands clasped in her lap. He bent to rest his elbows on his knees and ran his good hand over his face. He didn't want to open up any more than he already had until he knew where they stood. He wanted to ask her outright if she loved him and get to explanations later, yet part of him was afraid to hear the answer.

Still, he'd laid his heart bare last night, and, really, what did he have to lose?

Not a damn thing.

****

Texas swiped at her cheeks and tried to get control of her emotions. She'd been so happy, so excited to see Will and blurt out her feelings. But the second she'd seen him, all the fear and doubt bubbled up inside her and shut her down. This was Will. Super-hot, sexy, and every woman's dream. How could she be his?

Then she'd read the hurt and uncertainty in his sad brown eyes and lost it—again. She'd hurt him so much. Was still hurting him. "Will, it's okay. We don't have to—"

"No." He held up his injured hand. "Let me say this."

Letting his hands drop between his knees, he stared at the ground. "I guess I was content living in limbo, not getting anywhere with you, not even trying really but not moving on either. I honestly didn't think I stood a chance. And like you said, there was always the possibility I'd lose what little I had of you."

He sat back but didn't look at her. "I think I was hoping for things to change on your end. It wasn't until Jarod showed me the engagement ring that I realized what a fool I was. I'd waited too long." He laughed, though there was no humor in it. "You don't know how happy I was when you not only turned him down but broke it off. When I think about how close I came to losing you..." He shifted to face her. "I haven't, have I?"

Texas raised a hand to cup his stubbled jaw. "No, Will, you haven't. But you were wrong if you thought you could suddenly make me fall in love with you." She leaned forward and touched her lips to his. "I've loved you forever."

She started to kiss him again, but he tilted his head back. "Does that mean you believe me? That I love you?"

"Yes."

The deep V of his brows evened out, and some of the angst left his features. "And you trust me? No more talk of other women or greener pastures?"

Smiling, needing to see him smile, she shook her head. "Or horny bulls."

He closed his eyes and dropped his forehead to hers. His Adam's apple bobbed, the sound of it tugging at her heart.

"I'm so sorry I said all those things to you." She palmed his other cheek. "It's not that I didn't trust you. I just didn't trust myself. I was afraid I wanted it so much that I wasn't seeing the truth. And I was afraid if I let it be real, I'd lose you like I have everyone else. Then you left, and I was so alone. All I could think about was how much I needed to talk to you, my best friend. I needed you to tell me what to do. Then I realized you already had."

Black lashes lifted, and his eyes met hers. "I shouldn't have left."

"Just promise me you'll never do it again. No matter how stubborn and stupid I get."

"I promise." He lowered his mouth to hers in a gentle feathering. "I love you, T."

"I love you, too."

His arms wound around her, and she parted her lips to let his tongue inside. Heat bloomed in her belly. Her nipples grew taut, and little tingles spread through her breasts. She squirmed to get closer, but the swing tilted and she fell against his injured hand.

He broke the kiss on a wince, and she tried to pull away, but he growled low in his throat and hauled her onto his lap. His head lowered again, but she dodged his lips and pressed her hand against his chest. He still hadn't told her about his hand.

She ran a finger over the bandage holding the splint in place. "How bad is it?"

"Only fractured." He laid his arm along the back of the swing to get it out of harm's way. "I have to go back for a cast after the swelling goes down."

"Poor baby." She curled into him and kissed his neck. Moist with sweat, he tasted of salt. "You should see Jarod's face."

Will tensed beneath her. "He was here?"

The underlying tone in his voice made her smile. Not that she'd ever make him feel that way on purpose, but she kind of liked Will's jealousy. "He came to apologize."

"As he damn well should have." He grunted as if to put a stamp of approval on his assessment. Then he set the swing to rocking, slow and easy. The fingers of his left hand swept up and down her arm.

Contentment filled her from head to toe. "Does it hurt?"

"Some." He wiggled the only two digits visible. "But I'd do it again. I won't let anyone hurt you."

Did *anyone* include his mom? "Will?"

"Hmm?"

She licked her lips as if that would ease the

question from her mouth. The subject was a sore one. "What happened with your mom in Houston?"

The fingers stroking her arm stalled for a brief moment, then started up again. "Nothing you need to worry about."

Nope, no more secrets. "She wanted more money, didn't she? How much this time?"

"Does it matter?"

Maybe not, but… "She's why you sold Crusher, isn't she?"

"No. You are." His arm tightened around her. "When she's home, she causes trouble. She'd delight in finding some way to come between us. It was worth it to get her out of our lives."

So he *had* done it for her, for their future. She should be happy not to have to deal with Missy Sanderson, but all she felt was sad. For Will. In that moment, she vowed to do everything possible to make him happy, to show him what it truly meant to be loved.

The swing pitched as he suddenly brought it to a stop and urged her to sit up. "Come to my house tonight. I don't want us to waste another minute. I want you in my home, in my bed."

"Actually…" Texas bit her bottom lip. Would he think her presumptuous? She slid to her feet and crossed the porch to the front door. Reaching inside, she picked up the overnight bag she'd packed when she'd been certain they would work things out. She held it up for him to see.

He cocked his head to one side and lifted a brow. "Is that all you're taking?"

Dropping the luggage back inside and closing the door, she returned to stand in front of him and shrugged, a little nervous now that she'd put herself out there. "I didn't want to seem too sure of myself 'cause I sure as hell wasn't."

"Baby, if you come home with me, I'll never let you leave. Understand?"

The fire in his eyes made her skin blaze and her heart race. Had he always looked at her like that? "Yes."

"Good. Now, come here." He reached for her hand and tugged her closer.

Instead of sitting on his lap, she straddled his thighs, threaded her fingers through his hair, and bent to kiss him. His hands settled on her waist as her tongue teased his, circling the hot wet cavern of his mouth then retreating. He groaned and shifted her higher so that the thick ridge beneath his fly nudged her pussy.

Texas moaned against his lips and rocked her hips. Icy heat spread from her core, and she was sure he could feel her juices through his jeans. The thought only made her wetter.

"I have a confession to make." His deep rumble startled her from her sexual daze.

Easing back, she looked down at him. "Another one?"

What else could there be? And couldn't he wait until later to tell her?

"I lied earlier." He grinned. "Well, sort of."

She lifted a brow. "This is getting to be a habit with you."

His good hand left her waist and landed on her knee. His fingertips inched up her thigh. He watched their progression. "It's only a half lie."

She shivered and swayed forward a bit until her clit rasped against rough denim. Her pussy clenched, and she struggled to get the words out. "And that's better how?"

"Depends on you."

"Tell me, then." *And make it quick.*

"I didn't come here for sex, but if you keep this up, we aren't going to make it to my house."

Texas slid one hand down his chest, then over those sculpted abs to finally cup his cock. Her lips curled into a smile. "So, about that blowjob..."

Will's fingers dove under her skirt and along the underside of her ass until they skimmed her thong. He leaned forward to nip at her mouth. "So, about those hot pink panties..."

Epilogue

One month later...

As Will drove through the gate at the McNamara ranch, Texas lowered the visor mirror to apply a second coat of lip balm to her lips. Will had kissed off most of it when they'd stopped to pick up a peach cobbler from Faye's for the McNamara barbeque.

When Harper had invited her and Will out to Josh's for dinner, Texas thought it would just be the four of them, but this morning, Will mentioned talking to Evan about tax breaks and Kane about replacing Crusher. Now, she was nervous.

For the last month, she and Will had, other than while working, shut out the rest of the world. This was their first outing as a couple. They weren't hiding their relationship. They'd just been stingy with each other, making up for lost time.

Will darted a look at her over the top of his sunglasses. "If you don't want to stay, just give me a sign."

She closed the visor. "What kind of sign?"

Sitting back in the passenger seat, she let her gaze wander slowly over him without reservation. Something she'd never allowed herself to do in the past and thoroughly enjoyed over the last few weeks, especially knowing how much he liked it. He wore faded jeans, boots, and a pale yellow T-shirt that stretched across his chest. His sun-streaked brown hair stuck up in places where her fingers had been during the kiss they'd shared at the last stoplight out of town. She still couldn't believe he was hers.

His naughty grin sent her tummy tumbling. "Text me something sexy."

Texas reached over the console to smooth his hair. "Something like how I wish your mouth was on my..." She bit her lip and let his imagination fill in the rest.

He groaned. "Yes. Just like that." His gaze flicked over her breasts as the truck followed the gravel drive around Josh's house. "I'm half tempted to turn around and go home."

Home.

Texas was still getting used to calling Will's country mansion home. She'd lived in her parents' cozy little two-story farmhouse since she could remember, but wherever Will was, that was home.

"Too late," she said as Will pulled alongside the other guests' vehicles. She jutted her chin at the group of guys in lawn chairs under a newly erected gazebo. "They've already seen us."

Ignoring Will's stoic grumbling, Texas slid out of the truck and opened the back passenger door to grab the cobbler. As soon as she turned around and closed the door, he was there, crowding her against the hot panel.

Fingers splayed around her neck, his other hand

at her waist. He bent his head and brushed his mouth over hers. She surrendered to the kiss, opening for his tongue's seductive exploration. Her core contracted.

A moan escaped her throat as she melted into him, her free hand finding purchase in the silky hair at his nape. She arched against him just as his tongue eased from her mouth.

He stepped back and adjusted his hat. "*Now*, they've seen us."

Lacing his fingers with hers, he led her across the yard. Her legs felt like spaghetti, her face hot. She wasn't used to Will touching her in public. Not like this.

"Sorry we're late," he said to Josh who manned the grill.

"Grab a beer." Josh pointed to the ice chest then to the house. "Girls are all inside."

Texas nodded and turned away, but Will tugged on her hand until she looked up at him. His lips claimed hers in a quick kiss. "Love you."

"Love you, too," she whispered back.

Heart full, she was halfway across the yard before she caught movement in the kitchen window. More heat bloomed in her cheeks as she caught Harper's knowing smile.

As Texas entered the back door, her phone buzzed in her back pocket.

"Glad you could make it," Harper said from the sink, one flip-flopped foot crossed over the other. She pointed her beer bottle toward the far end of the table. "You know Shayna, right?"

Texas laid the pan of cobbler on the counter, pulled out her phone, and nodded at the willowy brunette with dark brown eyes that sparkled with contentment. "Yes. Hi, Shayna."

Texas had been ahead of Shayna in high school, but she remembered seeing her at parties down by the McNamara's lake the summer when Evan and Shayna hooked up. They'd been inseparable, the fiery chemistry almost combustible. Then suddenly, they weren't.

Her gaze dropped to her screen.

Will: *I miss you already.*

"And this is Bradi Montgomery." Harper indicated the other brunette at the table. "Bradi, Texas owns the auction barn in Stone Creek."

"It's nice to meet you." Texas stretched her hand across the table.

"You, too." Bradi shook her hand.

As soon as her hand was free, she returned Will's text.

Texas: *Miss you, too.*

She added a heart emoji.

This was what they did all day while Texas was working the barn and Will was busy with the ranch. More often than not, the texting turned naughty.

"She's the vet who inseminated Star last year," Harper continued, "and we're hoping she worked her magic on our new girl, Buttercup."

Bradi tipped a beer to her lips but stopped just shy of drinking. "Yeah, and Josh was paying close attention this time, so be careful. You might be next."

Beer sprayed from Harper's lips, a look of horror on her face as she coughed and shook her head. "Oh my god, no. I'm just getting used to this."

Harper held up her left hand. A diamond twinkled in the sunlight.

Shayna squealed and grabbed Harper's hand to inspect the engagement ring. "How did I not notice this? When did this happen?"

"A few weeks ago. We decided to announce it today so act surprised later when Josh makes his speech."

Texas moved closer to take a look at the ring, then shifted to peek out the window at Will. He'd been dropping hints of marriage but hadn't bit the bullet yet. Her answer would, of course, be yes, but as long as they were together, she'd wait for him to do the asking.

Ping.

Texas turned off the notification sound before reading the text.

Will: *Kane has a bull he's willing to let go of. Maybe we can go look at it sometime this week.*

Texas: *Sure.*

That he included her in the decision made her insides all warm and gooey. As if her opinion mattered. As if the ranch was theirs. As if they were married.

"Have you and Mason set a date?" Shayna asked Bradi, drawing Texas' attention back to the conversation.

"Not exactly." Bradi laughed. "He keeps asking me if I've changed my mind."

"Have you?" Shayna asked.

"No, I just want to keep it simple, and I know the moment we set a date, my mom will make a big deal out of it. I'm not that girl. Clay and Lindsey asked us to go to Vegas with them next month. I want to do it there. You know, come home with the deed already done so there's no fuss."

Bradi sounded like Texas' kind of girl. No fuss. No frills. Neither she nor Will had family so if he did ask, Texas wanted a small church wedding with only a few friends.

Josh knocked on the window over the sink. "Are the hamburger patties ready?"

"I'll bring them out," Harper said and moved to the fridge to pull out a platter of marinating beef patties. She set them on the table to remove the clingy wrap.

Shayna's chair scraped back as she stood and covered her mouth, her face pale. "Oh god."

She ran from the kitchen, Harper on her heels.

Texas looked at Bradi. "Is she…"

"That would be my guess." Bradi rose and started opening cabinets until she found what she was looking for. She placed a box of crackers on the table in front of Shayna's chair.

Texas curled her fingers into a fist to keep from touching her belly. She and Will hadn't been careful, and she was still on the pill, but that didn't stop the yearning to have their child growing there.

One thing at a time.

Her phone vibrated in her hand.

Will: *I'm hungry.*

What was she supposed to say to that?

Will: *For your pussy.*

Her clit twitched, and moisture dampened her panties. She could almost feel the rough pad of his tongue.

The screen door banged, making her jump like a naughty child.

Josh entered the kitchen. "I thought you were bringing—" His gaze searched the room, concern marring his brow. "Where's Harper? Everything okay?"

"Everything's fine." Texas set her phone down to hand him the tray of patties.

He looked at Bradi, who nodded to assure him. "Okay, these won't take long."

The second he left, Shayna walked into the kitchen on shaky legs, Harper holding her steady. Shayna lowered gingerly into her seat and dabbed a damp cloth to her cheeks.

Harper reached for the tray that wasn't there. Her eyes met Texas'.

Texas hooked her thumb over her shoulder toward the window. "Josh."

Nodding, Harper looked down at the phone next to the sink.

Shit. Texas snatched her phone and stuck it in her pocket. If she thought her face couldn't get any hotter, she was wrong.

Harper leaned close to whisper, "Is this what was going on at the town meeting last month?"

Texas groaned.

"Aren't you going to answer him?"

"Not yet, or we won't be around for burgers."

Harper chuckled and turned to Shayna. "How far along are you?"

"Just barely." Shayna nibbled on a cracker. "About ten weeks."

Bradi laughed. "I guess Evan was the one paying attention during the insemination."

"Does he know?" Harper asked.

"Yes, and he's been itching to tell everyone. I'm the one who wants to wait. At least until I'm through the first trimester."

"Has the morning sickness been bad?" Bradi asked.

Shayna shook her head. "But the freakin' smell of raw meat does it every time."

Harper snorted. "It's a good thing Josh is cooking, then. The last time Evan manned the grill, my burger was so bloody it mooed."

Shayna's face contorted. "Let's talk about something else."

Bradi sat forward. "Yeah, like who's the eye-candy without a plus one?"

Texas turned around to look out the window again. Who was Bradi talking about? Texas had been so flustered by Will's kiss, she'd only been aware of Josh and hadn't even noticed Evan or the other guy.

"That's Kane Kilbane," Harper said. "He has a ranch somewhere around Kerrville. Josh bought the new mare from him."

So that was the Kane Will mentioned buying a bull from. Brown hair, the color of dark chocolate, fell in waves around his face. His eyes were just as dark, penetrating in their intensity. The angles of his face were sharp. Long legs, trim hips, and broad shoulders, his body was made for sin and could probably make even the most devoted saint fall.

"He goes by Devil," Harper said.

Aptly fitting, but...

Texas turned back to ask, "Why?"

A look passed between Harper and Shayna, and Bradi seem to understand the silent communication, but Texas was left in the dark. She'd have to ask Will later.

"What do you think they're talking about?" Shayna asked, changing the subject. "My money's on football?"

"The price of beef," came from Bradi.

Harper snorted. "Josh can't talk about anything but Zephyr. That's what he named the foal."

"Will is looking for a young bull to replace Crusher," Texas offered her two cents.

Bradi laughed. "At least we know where we rank."

Before she'd met Harper, Texas would probably have fit in better outside talking about the same things as the men, but here she was, talking about engagements, weddings, and babies. Maybe it was because the women here were all strong and, with the exception of Shayna, worked jobs predominantly held by men. Or maybe it was because Will made her feel feminine and gave her all the things she didn't even know she wanted—love, a home, and family.

With Will, she had all three.

Harper pushed away from the sink and picked up a tray of condiments and paper goods. "Well, let's get out there and remind them we're here."

Carrying the cobbler she'd brought and a pitcher of sweet tea, Texas followed the others and helped arrange the tables set up as a buffet. When everything was ready except the burgers, she grabbed a beer and meandered over to perch on the wide, flat arm of the Adirondack chair Will occupied. She handed him the beer as his arm snaked around her, his hand settling on her hip.

Texas pulled out her phone, and without letting go of her, Will set the bottle aside and picked up his from where it lay on the other arm of the chair. She smiled and pretended to check her email.

He scrolled to his messages, looked up at her, and frowned. He lowered the phone to his thigh, and his knee began to bounce.

"Are you expecting a call?" Josh asked Will as he drew Harper against his side.

"Maybe," Will muttered.

Harper covered a laugh with a cough. "Sorry, I inhaled some beer earlier."

Taking pity on the man she loved, she thumbed a message.

Texas: *We can't leave until Josh makes an announcement.*

Will: *Ugh.*

Texas: *We had to come up for air some time.*

Will: *You can suffocate me any time.*

Texas leaned over to kiss his cheek. "You say the sweetest things."

"Sorry, I'm not very eloquent when I'm hungry," he said, pulling her onto his lap.

She palmed his cheek. "Eat a burger, drink some beer, and visit with your friends."

With his arms around her, she watched him type in the next text.

Will: *I'd rather eat you.*

Texas: *Don't worry, cowboy. You can eat all the pussy you want when we get home.*

Will nuzzled her ear. "You say the sweetest things."

Thank you for reading *Texas Two-Step*.

If you'd like to know more about Darah, her upcoming releases, and get a heads up about Devil's book, sign up for Darah's newsletter at *https://www.darahlace.com/newsletter/*

About Darah Lace...

Multi-published author of spicy contemporary and paranormal romance, Darah Lace lives in Texas where she enjoys a simple life with her husband and two dogs. She loves sports, music, watching a good romance, and penning scenes that sizzle. When she isn't writing, she's scouring bookstores for her next adventure.

Darah would love to hear from you at:
darah@darahlace.com
www.darahlace.com
www.linktr.ee/darahlace
https://www.amazon.com/author/darahlace
https://www.goodreads.com/darah_lace
https://www.bookbub.com/authors/darah-lace
https://www.tiktok.com/@darah_lace_author
www.instagram.com/darahlace/
www.facebook.com/darahlace
www.facebook.com/DarahLaceAuthor
https://twitter.com/DarahLace

Sign Up for Darah's Newsletter
https://www.darahlace.com/newsletter/

Also Available
If you enjoy a contemporary billionaire businessman with a Texas vibe, you might like…

Bachelor Unmasked
Preston Brothers Book One
By Darah Lace

He wears a disguise to discover the truth.
She wears one to keep secrets.

The last thing Spencer Preston wants is to attend a masquerade party. His plan? Get in and get out. However, an encounter with a hot she-devil changes his mind, especially when the woman behind the sequined mask is the prim and proper, no-nonsense, secretary he's been fighting an attraction to for months. Suspicious of her dual lifestyle, he slips on his mask and sets out to discover her secrets.

Melody Jamison hates hiding behind her plain-Jane persona, but her last job ended in sexual harassment. To get a promotion at Preston Enterprises, she needs to show Spencer she's more than a pretty face. The problem is, she's hot for her boss. When a friend suggests a masquerade might be the perfect place to let her hair down without revealing her secrets, she agrees to a night out. But she never dreams she'll meet a masked stranger who makes her body hum like only Spencer can.

There's a corporate spy running loose at Preston Enterprises, Melody is at the top of the suspect list, and Spencer must continue to hide behind a mask in order to uncover the truth.

If you like paranormal wolf shifters, you might like…
Claiming Sophia
MacTyre Valley Wolves Prequel
By Darah Lace

*He wants to claim her as his mate,
but being a shifter isn't his only secret…*

Sophia Reed has yet to find a way to get her growling college crush to make a move. He's put her in the friend zone even though the chemistry between them is hotter than the summer sun.

Brendan MacTyre aches to claim Sophia as his mate, but if telling her he is *mac tíre*—wolf—doesn't scare her away, discovering the secret that he must share her with his pack brothers might. And she's the one woman he doesn't want to share.

Other Books by Darah Lace

COWBOY ROUGH SERIES
Saddle Broke
Bucking Hard
End of His Rope
Taming the Wildcat
Texas Two-Step
Deal with the Devil (Coming 2025)

PRESTON BROTHERS SERIES
Bachelor Unmasked
Bachelor Auction
Bachelor Bad Boy (Coming Fall 2024)
Bachelor Betrayed (Coming 2025)

MACTYRE VALLEY WOLVES SERIES
Claiming Sophia
Embracing Everly (Coming 2025)

STAND ALONES
S.A.M.
Getting Lucky in London
Dragon's Bride
Yes, Master
Game Night
Wrong Number, Right Man
Yesterday's Desire

Printed in Great Britain
by Amazon